You Read to Me & I'll Read to You

20th-Century Stories to Share

selected by JANET SCHULMAN

Alfred A. Knopf ⚓ New York

For Valerie and Emerald

Many thanks to Susan Hirschman and Isabel Warren-Lynch
for their story suggestions and to Erin Clarke for all the help she gave me
in bringing this anthology to fruition

—J.S.

Cover illustration by William Steig first appeared on the cover of *Publishers Weekly* on July 18, 1994.

THIS IS A BORZOI BOOK PUBLISHED BY ALFRED A. KNOPF

Compilation copyright © 2001 by Janet Schulman
Cover, title page, copyright page, and A Note to Parents illustration copyright © 1994 by William Steig
Contents page illustrations copyright © 1940, renewed 1968 by Dr. Seuss Enterprises, L.P.;
copyright © 1971 by William Steig
Index illustration copyright © 1959 by Crockett Johnson
Published in the United States by Alfred A. Knopf, a division of Random House, Inc., New York,
and simultaneously in Canada by Random House of Canada Limited, Toronto.
Distributed by Random House, Inc., New York.
KNOPF, BORZOI BOOKS, and the colophon are registered trademarks of Random House, Inc.

Book design by Roberta Pressel
Hand-lettering by Jane Dill
Acknowledgments for permission to reproduce previously published material appear on page 250.

www.randomhouse.com/kids

Library of Congress Cataloging-in-Publication Data
You read to me and I'll read to you: 20th-century stories to share / compiled by Janet Schulman.
p. cm.
Includes index.
Summary: A collection of stories by such authors as Maurice Sendak, Roald Dahl, and Astrid Lindgren.
ISBN 0-375-81083-8
1. Children's stories. [1. Short stories.] I. Schulman, Janet.
PZ5.Y7   2001
[E]—dc21   2001029211

Printed in the United States of America
September 2001
10 9 8 7 6 5 4 3 2 1
First Edition

CONTENTS

A Note to Parents

I once read a story about a boy who tried to fool his mother into believing he could not learn to read. He was afraid those cherished nightly sessions of having her read to him would stop when he could read all by himself. Though the story was fictional, it is certainly true that most children continue to enjoy being read to long after they have mastered the skill themselves. And it is also generally true that the more children experience literature *worth* reading, the more they *want* to read.

Countless studies in recent years have proved that children who are frequently read to stand a much better chance of becoming lifelong lovers of books. Their verbal skills are enhanced and they usually do better in school. While many first-, second-, and third-grade teachers do read aloud to their class, your reading aloud at home is something special. It shows your child that you still care.

In 1998 I compiled *The 20th-Century Children's Book Treasury*. It presents classic picture books to be read aloud primarily to preschoolers. *You Read to Me & I'll Read to You* is a companion volume, but it is not more of the same. Rather, it is a step up. This anthology is for parents (or grandparents, older siblings, aunts, uncles, or baby-sitters) to share with children in the first few years of school, children who now can read. It's a sampler of many different types of stories written during the last seven decades of the twentieth century. For the most part the selections have more fully developed stories, with more words and fewer pictures, than those in *The 20th-Century Children's Book Treasury*. Some take just a few minutes to read, while others take about half an hour. Here you will find old friends, such as Dr. Seuss, William Steig, Edward Ardizzone, and Roald Dahl, and also exciting new ones for the school-age child.

All of the stories—short or long, humorous or thoughtful—are fun to read aloud. And there are so many different ways to approach the stories. Most are easy enough for children who can read books created with a "beginning to read" vocabulary. Maurice Sendak's *Pierre*, about a little boy who doesn't care, is a good one to start with. Its short, easy, rhymed story broken into very short "chapters" works well with alternating adult and child voices from chapter to chapter. Another very short, simple story in rhyme that works well read as a duet—you read one verse, your child reads the next—is *The Piggy in the Puddle* by Charlotte Pomerantz. It's a real tongue twister, and the faster you read it, the funnier it is, something your child can build up to after several readings.

The longer stories can be read all in one gulp or, if you want to keep the suspense going, a chapter a night. It could be your turn one night, your child's turn the next night. Or you read one page, your child reads the next. Few of us are trained readers. We may make little mistakes as we read aloud or struggle with some words from time to time. This is natural and can actually help your child to realize that it's okay to make mistakes reading aloud.

I believe these are satisfying stories that you and your child will want to hear again and again. They cover such a range of subjects and moods and settings and, while many were written decades ago, they remain fresh and true to the adventurous spirit of the young school-age child today. After you've read a few of the stories aloud, let your child decide which one to read the next time and gradually encourage his or her participation in the reading.

You don't have to be an expert to know how to use this book. Just leaf through it, read a few sentences, consider how many pages a story takes and whether it has many or few illustrations, and use your common sense. You know your child better than anyone!

—Janet Schulman
September 2001

AMOS & BORIS

written and illustrated by William Steig

Amos, a mouse, lived by the ocean. He loved the ocean. He loved the smell of sea air. He loved to hear the surf sounds—the bursting breakers, the backwashes with rolling pebbles.

He thought a lot about the ocean, and he wondered about the faraway places on the other side of the water. One day he started building a boat on the beach. He worked on it in the daytime, while at night he studied navigation.

When the boat was finished, he loaded it with cheese, biscuits, acorns, honey, wheat germ, two barrels of fresh water, a compass, a sextant, a telescope, a saw, a hammer and nails and some wood in case repairs should be necessary, a needle and thread for the mending of torn sails, and various other necessities such as bandages and iodine, a yo-yo and playing cards.

On the sixth of September, with a very calm sea, he waited till the high tide had almost reached his boat; then, using his most savage strength, he just managed to push the boat into the water, climb on board, and set sail.

The *Rodent,* for that was the boat's name, proved to be very well made and very well suited to the sea. And Amos, after one miserable day of seasickness, proved to be a natural sailor, very well suited to the ship.

He was enjoying his trip immensely. It was beautiful weather. Day and night he moved up and down, up and down, on waves as big as mountains, and he was full of wonder, full of enterprise, and full of love for life.

One night, in a phosphorescent sea, he marveled at the sight of some whales spouting luminous water; and later, lying on the deck of his boat gazing at the immense, starry sky, the tiny mouse Amos, a little speck of a living thing in the vast living universe, felt thoroughly akin to it all. Overwhelmed by the beauty and mystery of everything, he rolled over and over and right off the deck of his boat and into the sea.

"Help!" he squeaked as he grabbed desperately at the *Rodent*. But it evaded his grasp and went bowling along under full sail, and he never saw it again.

And there he was! Where? In the middle of the immense ocean, a thousand miles from the nearest shore, with no one else in sight as far as the eye could see and not even so much as a stick of driftwood to hold on to. "Should I try to swim home?" Amos wondered. "Or should I just try to stay afloat?" He might swim a 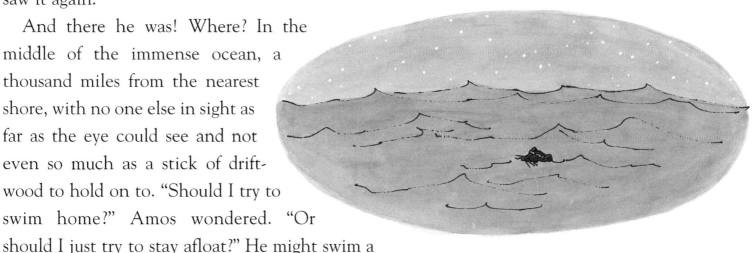 mile, but never a thousand. He decided to just keep afloat, treading water and hoping that something—who knows what?—would turn up to save him. But what if a shark, or some big fish, a horse mackerel, turned up? What was he supposed to do to protect himself? He didn't know.

Morning came, as it always does. He was getting terribly tired. He was a very small, very cold, very wet and worried mouse. There was still nothing in sight but the empty sea. Then, as if things weren't bad enough, it began to rain.

At last the rain stopped and the noonday sun gave him a bit of cheer and warmth in the vast loneliness; but his strength was giving out. He began to wonder what it would be like to drown. Would it take very long? Would it feel just awful? Would his soul go to heaven? Would there be other mice there?

As he was asking himself these dreadful questions, a huge head burst through the surface of the water and loomed up over him. It was a whale. "What sort of fish are you?" the whale asked. "You must be one of a kind!"

"I'm not a fish," said Amos. "I'm a mouse, which is a mammal, the highest form of life. I live on land."

"Holy clam and cuttlefish!" said the whale. "I'm a mammal myself, though I live in the sea. Call me Boris," he added.

Amos introduced himself and told Boris how he came to be there in the middle of the ocean. The whale said he would be happy to take Amos to the Ivory Coast of Africa, where he happened to be headed anyway, to attend a meeting of whales from all the seven seas. But Amos said he'd had enough adventure to last him a while. He wanted only to get back home and hoped the whale wouldn't mind going out of his way to take him there.

"Not only would I not mind," said Boris, "I would consider it a privilege. What other whale in all the world ever had the chance to get to know such a strange creature as you! Please climb aboard." And Amos got on Boris's back.

"Are you sure you're a mammal?" Amos asked. "You smell more like a fish." Then Boris the whale went swimming along, with Amos the mouse on his back.

What a relief to be so safe, so secure again! Amos lay down in the sun, and being worn to a frazzle, he was soon asleep.

Then all of a sudden he was in the water again, wide awake, spluttering and splashing about! Boris had forgotten for a moment that he had a passenger on his back and had sounded. When he realized his mistake, he surfaced so quickly that Amos was sent somersaulting, tail over whiskers, high into the air.

Hitting the water hurt. Crazy with rage, Amos screamed and punched at Boris until he remembered he owed his life to the whale and quietly climbed on his back. From then on, whenever Boris wanted to sound, he warned Amos in advance and got his okay, and whenever he sounded, Amos took a swim.

Swimming along, sometimes at great speed, sometimes slowly and

leisurely, sometimes resting and exchanging ideas, sometimes stopping to sleep, it took them a week to reach Amos's home shore. During that time, they developed a deep admiration for one another. Boris admired the delicacy, the quivering daintiness, the light touch, the small voice, the gemlike radiance of the mouse. Amos admired the bulk, the grandeur, the power, the purpose, the rich voice, and the abounding friendliness of the whale.

They became the closest possible friends. They told each other about their lives, their ambitions. They shared their deepest secrets with each other. The whale was very curious about life on land and was sorry that he could never experience it. Amos was fascinated by the whale's accounts of what went on deep under the sea. Amos sometimes enjoyed running up and down on the whale's back for exercise. When he was hungry, he ate plankton. The only thing he missed was fresh, unsalty water.

The time came to say goodbye. They were at the shore. "I wish we could be friends forever," said Boris. "We *will* be friends forever, but we can't be together. You must live on land and I must live at sea. I'll never forget you, though."

"And you can be sure I'll never forget *you*," said Amos. "I will always be grateful to you for saving my life and I want you to remember that if you ever need my help I'd be more than glad to give it!" How he could ever possibly help Boris, Amos didn't know, but he knew how willing he was.

The whale couldn't take Amos all the way in to land. They said their last goodbye and Amos dived off Boris's back and swam to the sand.

From the top of a cliff he watched Boris spout twice and disappear.

Boris laughed to himself. "How could that little mouse ever help me? Little as he is, he's all heart. I love him, and I'll miss him terribly."

Boris went to the conference off the Ivory Coast of Africa and then went back to a life of whaling about, while Amos returned to his life of mousing around. And they were both happy.

Many years after the incidents just described, when Amos was no longer a very young mouse, and when Boris was no longer a very young whale, there occurred one of the worst storms of the century, Hurricane Yetta; and it just so happened that Boris the whale was flung ashore by a tidal wave and stranded on the very shore where Amos happened to make his home.

It also just so happened that when the storm had cleared up and Boris was lying high and dry on the sand, losing his moisture in the hot sun and needing desperately to be back in the water, Amos came down to the beach to see how much damage Hurricane Yetta had done. Of course Boris and Amos recognized each other at once. I don't have to tell you how these old friends felt at meeting again in this desperate situation. Amos rushed toward Boris. Boris could only look at Amos.

"Amos, help me," said the mountain of a whale to the mote of a mouse. "I think I'll die if I don't get back in the water soon." Amos gazed at Boris in an agony of pity. He realized he had to do something very fast and had to think very fast about what it was he had to do. Suddenly he was gone.

"I'm afraid he won't be able to help me," said Boris to himself. "Much as he wants to do something, what can such a little fellow do?"

Just as Amos had once felt, all alone in the middle of the ocean, Boris felt now, lying alone on the shore. He was sure he would die. And just as he was preparing to die, Amos came racing back with two of the biggest elephants he could find.

Without wasting time, these two goodhearted elephants got to pushing with all their might at Boris's huge body until he began turning over, breaded with sand, and rolling down toward the sea. Amos, standing on the head of one of the elephants, yelled instructions, but no one heard him.

In a few minutes Boris was already in the water, with waves washing at him, and he was feeling the wonderful wetness. "You have to be out of the sea to really know how good it is to be in it," he thought. "That is, if you're a whale." Soon he was able to wiggle and wriggle into deeper water.

He looked back at Amos on the elephant's head. Tears were rolling down the great whale's cheeks. The tiny mouse had tears in his eyes too. "Goodbye, dear friend," squeaked Amos. "Goodbye, dear friend," rumbled Boris, and he disappeared in the waves. They knew they might never meet again. They knew they would never forget each other.

THE MAGIC FINGER

written by Roald Dahl
illustrated by Quentin Blake

The farm next to ours is owned by Mr. and Mrs. Gregg. The Greggs have two children, both of them boys. Their names are Philip and William. Sometimes I go over to their farm to play with them.

I am a girl and I am eight years old.

Philip is also eight years old.

William is three years older. He is ten.

What?

Oh, all right, then.

He is eleven.

Last week, something very funny happened to the Gregg family. I am going to tell you about it as best I can.

Now the one thing that Mr. Gregg and his two boys loved to do more than anything else was to go hunting. Every Saturday morning they would take their guns and go off into the woods to look for animals and birds to shoot. Even Philip, who was only eight years old, had a gun of his own.

I can't stand hunting. I just can't *stand* it. It doesn't seem right to me that men and boys should kill animals just for the fun they get out of it. So I used to try to stop Philip and William from doing it. Every time I went over to their farm I would do my best to talk them out of it, but they only laughed at me.

I even said something about it once to Mr. Gregg, but he just walked on past me as if I wasn't there.

Then, one Saturday morning, I saw Philip and William coming out of the woods with their father, and they were carrying a lovely young deer.

This made me so cross that I started shouting at them.

The boys laughed and made faces at me, and Mr. Gregg told me to go home and mind my own P's and Q's.

Well, that did it!

I saw red.

And before I was able to stop myself, I did something I never meant to do.

I PUT THE MAGIC FINGER ON THEM ALL!

Oh, dear! Oh, dear! I even put it on Mrs. Gregg, who wasn't there. I put it on the whole Gregg family.

For months I had been telling myself that I would never put the Magic Finger upon anyone again—not after what happened to my teacher, old Mrs. Winter.

Poor old Mrs. Winter.

One day we were in class, and she was teaching us spelling. "Stand up," she said to me, "and spell cat."

"That's an easy one," I said. "*K-a-t.*"

"You are a stupid little girl!" Mrs. Winter said.

"I am not a stupid little girl!" I cried. "I am a very nice little girl!"

"Go and stand in the corner," Mrs. Winter said.

Then I got cross, and I saw red, and I put the Magic Finger on Mrs. Winter good and strong, and almost at once . . .

Guess what?

Whiskers began growing out of her face! They were long black whiskers, just like the ones you see on a cat, only much bigger. And how

fast they grew! Before we had time to think, they were out to her ears!

Of course the whole class started screaming with laughter, and then Mrs. Winter said, "Will you be so kind as to tell me what you find so madly funny, all of you?"

And when she turned around to write something on the blackboard we saw that she had grown a *tail* as well! It was a huge bushy tail!

I cannot begin to tell you what happened after that, but if any of you are wondering whether Mrs. Winter is quite all right again now, the answer is No. And she never will be.

The Magic Finger is something I have been able to do all my life.

I can't tell you just *how* I do it, because I don't even know myself.

But it always happens when I get cross, when I see red . . .

Then I get very, very hot all over . . .

Then the tip of the forefinger of my right hand begins to tingle most terribly . . .

And suddenly a sort of flash comes out of me, a quick flash, like something electric.

It jumps out and touches the person who has made me cross . . .

And after that the Magic Finger is upon him or her, and things begin to happen . . .

Well, the Magic Finger was now upon the whole of the Gregg family, and there was no taking it off again.

I ran home and waited for things to happen.

They happened fast.

I shall now tell you what those things were. I got the whole story from Philip and William the next morning, after it was all over.

In the afternoon of the very same day that I put the Magic Finger on the Gregg family, Mr. Gregg and Philip and William went out hunting once again. This time they were going after wild ducks, so they headed towards the lake.

In the first hour they got ten birds.

In the next hour they got another six.

"What a day!" cried Mr. Gregg. "This is the best yet!" He was beside himself with joy.

Just then four more wild ducks flew over their heads. They were flying very low. They were easy to hit.

BANG! BANG! BANG! BANG! went the guns.

The ducks flew on.

"We missed!" said Mr. Gregg. "That's funny."

Then, to everyone's surprise, the four ducks turned around and came flying right back to the guns.

"Hey!" said Mr. Gregg. "What on earth are they doing? They are really asking for it this time!" He shot at them again. So did the boys. And again they all missed!

Mr. Gregg got very red in the face. "It's the light," he said. "It's getting too dark to see. Let's go home."

So they started for home, carrying with them the sixteen birds they had shot before.

But the four ducks would not leave them alone. They now began flying around and around the hunters as they walked away.

Mr. Gregg did not like it one bit. "Be off!" he cried, and he shot at them many more times, but it was no good. He simply could not hit them. All the way home those four ducks flew around in the sky above their heads, and nothing would make them go away.

Late that night, after Philip and William had gone to bed, Mr. Gregg went outside to get some wood for the fire.

He was crossing the yard when all at once he heard the call of a wild duck in the sky.

He stopped and looked up. The night was very still. There was a thin yellow moon over the trees on the hill, and the sky was filled with stars. Then Mr. Gregg heard the noise of wings flying low over his head, and he saw the four ducks, dark against the night sky, flying very close together. They were going around and around the house.

Mr. Gregg forgot about the firewood, and hurried back indoors. He was now quite afraid. He did not like what was going on. But he said nothing about it to Mrs. Gregg. All he said was, "Come on, let's go to bed. I feel tired."

So they went to bed and to sleep.

When morning came, Mr. Gregg was the first to wake up.

He opened his eyes.

He was about to put out a hand for his watch, to see the time.

But his hand wouldn't come out.

"That's funny," he said. "Where is my hand?"

He lay still, wondering what was up.

Maybe he had hurt that hand in some way?

He tried the other hand.

That wouldn't come out either.

He sat up.

Then, for the first time, he saw what he looked like!

He gave a yell and jumped out of bed.

Mrs. Gregg woke up. And when she saw Mr. Gregg standing there on the floor, *she* gave a yell, too.

For he was now a tiny little man!

He was maybe as tall as the seat of a chair, but no taller.

And where his arms had been, he had a pair of duck's wings instead!

"But . . . but . . . but . . ." cried Mrs. Gregg, going purple in the face. "My dear man, what's happened to you?"

"What's happened to both of us, you mean!" shouted Mr. Gregg.

It was Mrs. Gregg's turn now to jump out of bed.

She ran to look at herself in the glass. But she was not tall enough to see into it. She was even smaller than Mr. Gregg, and she, too, had got wings instead of arms.

"Oh! Oh! Oh! Oh!" sobbed Mrs. Gregg.

"This is witches' work!" cried Mr. Gregg. And both of them started running around the room, flapping their wings.

A minute later Philip and William burst in. The same thing had happened to them. They had wings and no arms. And they were *really* tiny. They were about as big as robins.

"Mama! Mama! Mama!" chirruped Philip. "Look, Mama, we can fly!" And they flew up into the air.

"Come down at once!" said Mrs. Gregg. "You're much too high!" But before she could say another word, Philip and William had flown right out the window.

Mr. and Mrs. Gregg ran to the window and looked out. The two tiny boys were now high up in the sky.

Then Mrs. Gregg said to Mr. Gregg, "Do you think *we* could do that, my dear?"

"I don't see why not," Mr. Gregg said. "Come on, let's try."

Mr. Gregg began to flap his wings hard, and all at once, up he went. Then Mrs. Gregg did the same.

"Help!" she cried as she started going up. "Save me!"

"Come on," said Mr. Gregg. "Don't be afraid."

So out the window they flew, far up into the sky, and it did not take them long to catch up with Philip and William.

Soon the whole family was flying around and around together.

"Oh, isn't it lovely!" cried William. "I've always wanted to know what it feels like to be a bird!"

"Your wings are not getting tired, are they, dear?" Mr. Gregg asked Mrs. Gregg.

"Not at all," Mrs. Gregg said. "I could go on forever!"

"Hey, look down there!" said Philip. "Somebody is walking in our garden!"

They all looked down, and there below them, in their own garden, they saw four *enormous* wild ducks! The ducks were as big as men, and what is more, they had great long arms, like men, instead of wings.

The ducks were walking in a line to the door of the Greggs' house, swinging their arms and holding their beaks high in the air.

"Stop!" called the tiny Mr. Gregg, flying down low over their heads. "Go away! That's my house!"

The ducks looked up and quacked. The first one put out a hand and opened the door of the house and went in. The others went in after him. The door shut.

The Greggs flew down and sat on the wall near the door. Mrs. Gregg began to cry.

"Oh, dear! Oh, dear!" she sobbed. "They have taken our house. What *shall* we do? We have no place to go!"

Even the boys began to cry a bit now.

"We will be eaten by cats and foxes in the night!" said Philip.

"I want to sleep in my own bed!" said William.

"Now then," said Mr. Gregg. "It isn't any good crying. That won't help us. Shall I tell you what we are going to do?"

"What?" they said.

Mr. Gregg looked at them and smiled. "We are going to build a nest."

"A nest!" they said. "Can we do that?"

"We *must* do it," said Mr. Gregg. "We've got to have somewhere to sleep. Follow me."

They flew off to a tall tree, and right at the top of it Mr. Gregg chose the place for the nest.

"Now we want sticks," he said. "Lots and lots of little sticks. Off you go, all of you, and find them and bring them back here."

"But we have no hands!" said Philip.

"Then use your mouths."

Mrs. Gregg and the children flew off. Soon they were back, carrying sticks in their mouths.

Mr. Gregg took the sticks and started to build the nest.

"More," he said. "I want more and more and more sticks. Keep going."

The nest began to grow. Mr. Gregg was very good at making the sticks stick together.

After a while he said, "That's enough sticks. Now I want leaves and feathers and things like that to make the inside nice and soft."

The building of the nest went on and on. It took a long time. But at last it was finished.

"Try it," said Mr. Gregg, hopping back. He was very pleased with his work.

"Oh, isn't it lovely!" cried Mrs. Gregg, going into it and sitting down. "I feel I might lay an egg any moment!"

The others all got in beside her.

"How warm it is!" said William.

"And what fun to be living so high up," said Philip. "We may be small, but nobody can hurt us up here."

"But what about food?" said Mrs. Gregg. "We haven't had a thing to eat all day."

"That's right," Mr. Gregg said. "So we will now fly back to the house and go in by an open window and get the tin of biscuits when the ducks aren't looking."

"Oh, we will be pecked to bits by those dirty great ducks!" cried Mrs. Gregg.

"We shall be very careful, my love," said Mr. Gregg. And off they went.

But when they got to the house, they found all the windows and doors closed. There was no way in.

"Just look at that beastly duck cooking at my stove!" cried Mrs. Gregg as she flew past the kitchen window. "How dare she!"

"And look at *that* one holding my lovely gun!" shouted Mr. Gregg.

"One of them is lying in my bed!" yelled William, looking into a top window.

"And one of them is playing with my electric train!" cried Philip.

"Oh, dear! Oh, dear!" said Mrs. Gregg. "They have taken over our whole house! We shall never get it back. And what *are* we going to eat?"

"I will *not* eat worms," said Philip. "I would rather die."

"Or slugs," said William.

Mrs. Gregg took the two boys under her

wings and hugged them. "Don't worry," she said.

"I can mince it all up very fine and you won't even know the difference. Lovely slugburgers. Delicious wormburgers."

"Oh no!" cried William.

"Never!" said Philip.

"Disgusting!" said Mr. Gregg. "Just because we have wings, we don't have to eat bird food. We shall eat apples instead. Our trees are full of them. Come on!"

So they flew off to an apple tree.

But to eat an apple without holding it in your hands is not at all easy. Every time you try to get your teeth into it, it just pushes away. In the end, they were able to get a few small bites each. And then it began to get dark, so they all flew back to the nest and lay down to sleep.

It must have been at about this time that I, back in my own house, picked up the telephone and tried to call Philip. I wanted to see if the family was all right.

"Hello," I said.

"Quack!" said a voice at the other end.

"Who is it?" I asked.

"Quack-quack!"

"Philip," I said, "is that you?"

"Quack-quack-quack-quack-quack!"

"Oh, stop it!" I said.

Then there came a very funny noise. It was like a bird laughing.

I put down the telephone quickly.

"Oh, that Magic Finger!" I cried. "What *has* it done to my friends?"

That night, while Mr. and Mrs. Gregg and Philip and William were trying to get some sleep up in the high nest, a great wind began to blow.

The tree rocked from side to side, and everyone, even Mr. Gregg, was afraid that the nest would fall down. Then came the rain. It rained and rained, and the water ran into the nest and they all got as wet as could be—and oh, it was a bad, bad night!

At last the morning came, and with it the warm sun.

"Well!" said Mrs. Gregg. "Thank goodness that's over! I never want to sleep in a nest again!" She got up and looked over the side . . .

"Help!" she cried. "Look! Look down there!"

"What is it, my love?" said Mr. Gregg. He stood up and peeped over the side.

He got the surprise of his life!

On the ground below them stood the four enormous ducks, as tall as men, and three of them were holding guns in their hands. One had Mr. Gregg's gun, one had Philip's gun, and one had William's gun.

The guns were all pointing right up at the nest.

"No! No! No!" called out Mr. and Mrs. Gregg, both together. "Don't shoot! Please don't shoot!"

"Why not?" said one of the ducks. It was the one who wasn't holding a gun. "You are always shooting at *us*."

"Oh, but that's not the same!" said Mr. Gregg. "We are *allowed* to shoot ducks!"

"Who allows you?" asked the duck.

"We allow each other," said Mr. Gregg.

"Very nice," said the duck. "And now *we* are going to allow each other to shoot you."

(I would have loved to have seen Mr. Gregg's face just then.)

"Oh, *please!*" cried Mrs. Gregg. "My two little children are up here with us! You wouldn't shoot my *children!*"

"Yesterday you shot *my* children," said the duck. "You shot all six of my children."

"I'll never do it again!" cried Mr. Gregg. "Never, never, never!"

"Do you really mean that?" asked the duck.

"I *do* mean it!" said Mr. Gregg. "I'll never shoot another duck as long as I live."

"That is not good enough," said the duck. "What about deer?"

"I'll do anything you say if you will only put down those guns!" cried Mr. Gregg. "I'll never shoot another duck or another deer or anything else again!"

"Will you give me your word on that?" said the duck.

"I will! I will!" said Mr. Gregg.

"Will you throw away your guns?" asked the duck.

"I will break them into tiny bits!" said Mr. Gregg. "And never again need you be afraid of me or my family."

"Very well," said the duck. "You may now come down. And by the way, may I congratulate you on the nest. For a first effort it's pretty good."

Mr. and Mrs. Gregg and Philip and William hopped out of the nest and flew down.

Then all at once everything went black before their eyes, and they couldn't see. At the same time a funny feeling came over them all, and they heard a great wind blowing in their ears.

Then the black that was before their eyes turned to blue, to green, to red, and then to gold, and suddenly, there they were, standing in lovely bright sunshine in their own garden, near their own house, and everything was back to normal once again.

"Our wings have gone!" cried Mr. Gregg. "And our arms have come back!"

"And we are not tiny anymore!" laughed Mrs. Gregg. "Oh, I am so glad!"

Philip and William began dancing about with joy.

Then, high above their heads, they heard the call of a wild duck. They all looked up, and they saw the four birds, lovely against the blue sky, flying very close together, heading back to the lake in the woods.

It must have been about half an hour later that I myself walked into the Greggs' garden. I had come to see how things were going, and I must admit I was expecting the worst. At the gate I stopped and stared. It was a queer sight.

In one corner Mr. Gregg was smashing all three guns into tiny pieces with a huge hammer.

In another corner Mrs. Gregg was placing beautiful flowers upon sixteen tiny mounds of soil, which I learned later were the graves of the ducks that had been shot the day before.

And in the middle of the yard stood Philip and William, with a sack of their father's best barley beside them. They were surrounded by ducks, doves, pigeons, sparrows, robins, larks, and many other kinds that I did not know, and the birds were eating the barley that the boys were scattering by the handful.

"Good morning, Mr. Gregg," I said.

Mr. Gregg lowered his hammer and looked at me. "My name is not Gregg anymore," he said. "In honor of my feathered friends, I have changed it from Gregg to Egg."

"And I am Mrs. Egg," said Mrs. Gregg.

"What happened?" I asked. They seemed to have gone completely dotty, all four of them.

Philip and William then began to tell me the whole story. When they had finished, William said, "Look! There's the nest! Can you see it? Right up in the top of the tree! That's where we slept last night!"

"I built it *all* myself," Mr. Egg said proudly. "Every stick of it."

"If you don't believe us," Mrs. Egg said, "just go into the house and take a look at the bathroom. It's a mess."

"They filled the tub right up to the brim," Philip said. "They must have been swimming around in it all night! And feathers everywhere!"

"Ducks like water," Mr. Egg said. "I'm glad they had a good time."

Just then, from somewhere over by the lake, there came a loud BANG!

"Someone's shooting!" I cried.

"That'll be Jim Cooper," Mr. Egg said. "Him and his three boys. They're shooting mad, those Coopers are, the whole family."

Suddenly I started to see red . . .

Then I got very hot all over . . .

Then the tip of my finger began tingling most terribly. I could feel the power building up and up inside me . . .

I turned and started running towards the lake as fast as I could.

"Hey!" shouted Mr. Egg. "What's up? Where are you going?"

"To find the Coopers," I called back.

"But why?"

"You wait and see!" I said. "They'll be nesting in the trees tonight, every one of them!"

THE PIGGY IN THE PUDDLE

written by Charlotte Pomerantz
illustrated by James Marshall

See the piggy,
See the puddle,
See the muddy little puddle.
See the piggy in the middle
Of the muddy little puddle.
See her dawdle, see her diddle
In the muddy, muddy middle.
See her waddle, plump and little,
In the very merry middle.

See her daddy,
Fuddy-duddy, fuddy-duddy, fuddy-duddy.
"Don't you get all muddy,
Muddy, muddy, muddy, muddy.
You are much too plump and little
To be in the muddy middle.
Mud is squishy, mud is squashy,
Mud is oh so squishy-squashy.
What you need is lots of soap."
But the piggy answered,
"Squishy-squashy, squishy-squashy—NOPE!"

See her mommy,
Fiddle-faddle, fiddle-faddle, fiddle-faddle.
"Get out of there—skedaddle,
Daddle, daddle, daddle, daddle.
You are much too plump and little
To be in the muddy middle.
Mud is mooshy, mud is squooshy,
Mud is oh so mooshy-squooshy.
What you need is lots of soap."
But the piggy answered,
"Mooshy-squooshy, mooshy-squooshy—NOPE!"

See her brother,
Silly billy, silly billy, silly billy.
"Do not waddle willy-nilly,
Willy-nilly, willy-nilly.
You are much too plump and little
To be in the muddy middle.
Mud is oofy, mud is poofy,
Mud is oh so oofy-poofy.
What you need is lots of soap."

But the piggy answered,
"Oofy-poofy, oofy-poofy—NOPE!"

The Piggy in the Puddle   27

Now they all stood in a huddle,
Right beside the muddy puddle.
And they looked into the puddle—
What a muddy, muddy muddle!

There was a piggy, plump and little,
In the very merry middle.
She was waddling, she was paddling,
She was diving way down derry.
She was wiggling, she was giggling,
She was very, very merry.
Said the mother,
"Little piggy, you have made me very mad."
Said the father,
"Little piggy, you have made me very sad."
"Little piggy," said the brother,
"You are very, very bad."
Said the piggy,
"Squishy-squashy, mooshy-squooshy, very bad."

"Dear, oh dear," said piggy's mother.
"What's a mother pig to do?"
She thought and thought and thought and thought—
And then, of course, she knew.
She said, "I bet my feet get wet."
And—jumped—in—too!

See two piggies in the puddle,
In the muddy little puddle.
See the piggy and her mommy
In the muddy little puddle.
"Me oh my," said piggy's father.
"What's a father pig to do?"
He thought and thought and thought and thought—
And then, of course, he knew.
He said, "I bet my tail gets wet."
And—jumped—in—too!

See three piggies in the puddle,
In the muddy little puddle.
See mommy, daddy, piggy
In the muddy little puddle.
"Boo-hoo-hoo," cried piggy's brother.
"Whatever shall I do?"
He thought, but not for very long,
Because, of course, he knew.
He held his nose and yelled, "Here goes!"
And—jumped—in—too!

The Piggy in the Puddle

See four piggies in the puddle,
In the muddy little puddle.
See the piggies in the middle
Of the muddy little puddle.
See them diddle, big and little,
In the very merry middle.
Said the daddy, "Mud is squishy,
Mud is oh so squishy-squashy."
Said the mommy, "Mud is mooshy,
Mud is oh so mooshy-squooshy."
Said the brother, "Mud is oofy,
Mud is oh so oofy-poofy."

Said the piggy,
"Squishy-squashy, mooshy-squooshy, oofy-poofy.
Indeed," said little piggy,
"I think we need some soap."
But the other piggies answered,
"Oofy-poofy—NOPE!"

So they all dove way down derry,
And were very, very merry.

The Tenth Good Thing
About Barney

written by Judith Viorst
illustrated by Erik Blegvad

My cat Barney died last Friday.
I was very sad.

I cried, and I didn't
watch television.
I cried, and I didn't eat my chicken or even the chocolate pudding.
I went to bed, and I cried.

My mother sat down on my bed, and she gave me a hug.
She said we could have a funeral for Barney in the morning.
She said I should think of ten good things about Barney so I could tell
them at the funeral.

I thought, and I thought, and I thought of good things about Barney.
I thought of nine good things. Then I fell asleep.

In the morning my mother wrapped Barney in a yellow scarf.
My father buried Barney in the ground by a tree in the yard.
Annie, my friend from next door, came over with flowers.
And I told good things about Barney.

Barney was brave, I said.
And smart and funny and clean.
Also cuddly and handsome, and he only once ate a bird.
It was sweet, I said, to hear him purr in my ear.
And sometimes he slept on my belly and kept it warm.

Those are all good things, said my mother, but I just count nine.
I said I would try to think of another one later.

At the end of the funeral we sang a song for Barney.

We couldn't remember any cat songs, so we sang one about
a pussywillow.
Even my father knew the words.

Then Annie and I went into the kitchen with
Mother.
She gave us orangeade and butter cookies, and she
left the box on the table so we could have seconds.
I gave my seconds to Annie. I miss Barney, I said.

Annie said Barney was in heaven with lots of cats
and angels, drinking cream and eating cans of tuna.

I said Barney was in the ground.

Heaven, said Annie, heaven. So there! The ground, I told her, the
ground. You don't know anything.

My father came in from the yard and took a cookie.
Big-mouthed Annie said heaven again. I said ground.
Tell her who's right, I asked Father. She doesn't know anything.

Maybe Barney's in heaven, my father began.
Aha, said Annie, and stuck her tongue out at me.

And maybe, said my father, Barney isn't.
What did I tell you, I said, and yanked Annie's braid.

Father made me let go.
We don't know too much about heaven, he told Annie.
We can't be absolutely sure that it's there.

But if it is there, said Annie in her absolutely sure voice, it's bound to
have room for Barney and tuna and cream.
She finished another cookie and went back home.

The Tenth Good Thing About Barney 33

My father told me he had to work in the garden.
I said that I would help—but only a little.
I told him I didn't like it that Barney was dead.

He said, why should I like it? It's sad, he said.
He told me that it might not feel so sad tomorrow.

My father had a packet of little brown seeds.
He shook some out on his hand.
The ground will give them food and a place to live, he said.
And soon they'll grow a stem and some leaves and flowers.

I squeezed the packet open and looked down to the bottom.
I told him, I don't see leaves and I don't see flowers.

Things change in the ground, said my father.
In the ground everything changes.

Will Barney change too? I asked him.

Oh yes, said my father.
He'll change until he's part of the ground in the garden.

And then, I asked, will he help to make flowers and leaves?

He will, said my father.
He'll help grow the flowers, and he'll help grow that tree and some grass.
You know, he said, that's a pretty nice job for a cat.

My father and I planted all of the seeds in the garden.
Mother made sandwiches, and we ate them under the tree.
After lunch we worked in the garden some more.

At night I still didn't want to watch any television.
When I turned out the light, my mother sat down on my bed.
She gave me a hug, and I said I had something to tell her.
Listen, I said, and I told the good things about Barney.

Barney was brave, I said.
And smart and funny and clean.
Also cuddly and handsome, and he only once ate a bird.
It was sweet, I said, to hear him purr in my ear.
And sometimes he slept on my belly and kept it warm.

Those are all good things, said my mother, but I still just count nine.

Yes, I said, but now I have another.

Barney is in the ground and he's helping grow flowers.
You know, I said, that's a pretty nice job for a cat.

Horton Hatches the Egg

written and illustrated by Dr. Seuss

Sighed Mayzie, a lazy bird hatching an egg:
"I'm tired and I'm bored
And I've kinks in my leg
From sitting, just sitting here day after day.
It's *work!* How I hate it!
I'd *much* rather play!
I'd take a vacation, fly off for a rest
If I could find *someone* to stay on my nest!

If I could find someone, I'd fly away—free. . . ."

Then Horton, the Elephant, passed by her tree.

"Hello!" called the lazy bird, smiling her best,
"You've nothing to do and I *do* need a rest.
Would YOU like to sit on the egg in my nest?"

The elephant laughed.
"Why, of all silly things!
I haven't feathers and *I* haven't wings.
ME on your egg? Why, that doesn't make sense. . . .
Your egg is so small, ma'am, and I'm so immense!"

"Tut, tut," answered Mayzie. "I know you're not small
But I'm *sure* you can do it. No trouble at all.
Just sit on it softly. You're gentle and kind.
Come, be a good fellow. I know you won't mind."

"I can't," said the elephant.
"PL-E-E-ASE!" begged the bird.

"I won't be gone long, sir. I give you my word.
I'll hurry right back. Why, I'll never be missed. . . ."

"Very well," said the elephant, "since you insist. . . .
You want a vacation. Go fly off and take it.
I'll sit on your egg and I'll try not to break it.
I'll stay and be faithful. I mean what I say."

"Toodle-oo!" sang out Mayzie and fluttered away.

"H-m-m-m . . . the first thing to do," murmured Horton,
"Let's see. . . .
The first thing to do is to prop up this tree
And make it much stronger. That *has* to be done
Before I get on it. I must weigh a ton."

Then carefully,
Tenderly,
Gently he crept
Up the trunk to the nest where the little egg slept.

Then Horton the Elephant smiled. "Now that's that. . . ."

    And he sat

                and he sat

                          and he sat

                                    and he sat. . . .

And he sat all that day
And he kept the egg warm. . . .
And he sat all that night
Through a *terrible* storm.
It poured and it lightninged!
It thundered! It rumbled!
"This isn't much fun,"
The poor elephant grumbled.
"I wish she'd come back
'Cause I'm cold and I'm wet.
I hope that that Mayzie bird doesn't forget."

But Mayzie, by this time, was far beyond reach,
Enjoying the sunshine way off in Palm Beach,
And having *such* fun, such a wonderful rest,

Decided she'd NEVER go back to her nest!

So Horton kept sitting there, day after day.
And soon it was Autumn. The leaves blew away.
And then came the Winter . . . the snow and the sleet!
And icicles hung
From his trunk and his feet.

But Horton kept sitting, and said with a sneeze,
"I'll *stay* on this egg and I *won't* let it freeze.
I meant what I said
And I said what I meant. . . .
An elephant's faithful
One hundred per cent!"

So poor Horton sat there
The whole winter through. . . .
And then came the springtime
With troubles anew!
His friends gathered round
And they shouted with glee.

"Look! Horton the Elephant's
Up in a tree!"
They taunted. They teased him.
They yelled, "How absurd!"
"Old Horton the Elephant
Thinks he's a bird!"

They laughed and they laughed. Then they all ran away.
And Horton was lonely. He wanted to play.
But he sat on the egg and continued to say:
"I meant what I said
And I said what I meant. . . .
An elephant's faithful
One hundred per cent!

"No matter WHAT happens,
This egg must be tended!"

But poor Horton's troubles
Were far, far from ended.
For, while Horton sat there
So faithful, so kind,
Three hunters came sneaking
Up softly behind!

He heard the men's footsteps!
He turned with a start!
Three rifles were aiming
Right straight at his heart!

Did he run?
He did not!
HORTON STAYED ON THAT NEST!
He held his head high
And he threw out his chest
And he looked at the hunters
As much as to say:
"Shoot if you must
But I *won't* run away!
I meant what I said
And I said what I meant. . . .
An elephant's faithful
One hundred per cent!"

But the men *didn't* shoot!
Much to Horton's surprise,
They dropped their three guns
And they stared with wide eyes!
"Look!" they all shouted,
"Can such a thing be?
An elephant sitting on top of a tree . . ."

"It's strange! It's amazing! It's wonderful! New!
Don't shoot him. We'll CATCH him. That's *just* what we'll do!
Let's take him alive. Why, he's terribly funny!
We'll sell him back home to a circus, for money!"

And the first thing he knew, they had built a big wagon
With ropes on the front for the pullers to drag on.
They dug up his tree and they put it inside,
With Horton so sad that he practically cried.
"We're off!" the men shouted. And off they all went
With Horton unhappy, one hundred per cent.

Up out of the jungle! Up into the sky!
Up over the mountains ten thousand feet high!
Then down, down the mountains
And down to the sea
Went the cart with the elephant,
Egg, nest and tree . . .

Then out of the wagon
And onto a ship!
Out over the ocean . . .
And oooh, what a trip!
Rolling and tossing and splashed with the spray!
And Horton said, day after day after day,
"I meant what I said
And I said what I meant. . . .
But oh, am I seasick!
One hundred per cent!"

After bobbing around for two weeks like a cork,
They landed at last in the town of New York.
"All ashore!" the men shouted,
And down with a lurch
Went Horton the Elephant
Still on his perch,
Tied onto a board that could just scarcely hold him. . . .

BUMP!

Horton landed!

And then the men sold him!

Sold to a circus! Then week after week

They showed him to people at ten cents a peek.

They took him to Boston, to Kalamazoo,

Chicago, Weehawken and Washington, too;

To Dayton, Ohio; St. Paul, Minnesota;

To Wichita, Kansas; to Drake, North Dakota.

And everywhere thousands of folks flocked to see

And laugh at the elephant up in a tree.

Poor Horton grew sadder the farther he went,

But he said as he sat in the hot noisy tent:

"I meant what I said, and I said what I meant. . . .

An elephant's faithful—one hundred per cent!"

Horton Hatches the Egg   49

Then . . . ONE DAY
The Circus Show happened to reach
A town way down south, not so far from Palm Beach.
And, dawdling along way up high in the sky,
Who (*of all people!*) should chance to fly by
But that old good-for-nothing bird, runaway Mayzie!
Still on vacation and still just as lazy.
And, spying the flags and the tents just below,
She sang out, "What fun! Why, I'll go to the show!"

And she swooped from the clouds
Through an open tent door . . .
"*Good gracious!*" gasped Mayzie,
"*I've seen* YOU *before!*"

Poor Horton looked up with his face white as chalk!
He started to speak, but before he could talk . . .

There rang out the noisiest ear-splitting squeaks
From the egg that he'd sat on for fifty-one weeks!
A thumping! A bumping! A wild alive scratching!
"My *egg!*" shouted Horton. "My EGG! WHY, IT'S HATCHING!"

"But it's MINE!" screamed the bird, when she heard the egg crack.
(The work was all done. Now she wanted it back.)
"It's MY egg!" she sputtered. "You stole it from me!
Get off of my nest and get out of my tree!"

Poor Horton backed down
With a sad, heavy heart. . . .

But at that very instant, the egg burst apart!
And out of the pieces of red and white shell,
From the egg that he'd sat on so long and so well,
Horton the Elephant saw something whizz!
IT HAD EARS

AND A TAIL

AND A TRUNK JUST LIKE HIS!

And the people came shouting, *"What's all this about . . . ?"*
They looked! And they stared with their eyes popping out!
Then they cheered and they *cheered* and they CHEERED more and more.
They'd never seen anything like it before!
"My goodness! *My gracious!*" they shouted. "MY WORD!
It's something brand new!
IT'S AN ELEPHANT-BIRD!!

And it should be, it *should* be, it SHOULD be like that!

Because Horton was faithful! He sat and he sat!

He meant what he said

And he said what he meant. . . ."

. . . And they sent him home
Happy,
One hundred per cent!

THE SHRINKING OF TREEHORN

written by Florence Parry Heide
illustrated by Edward Gorey

Something very strange was happening to Treehorn.

The first thing he noticed was that he couldn't reach the shelf in his closet that he had always been able to reach before, the one where he hid his candy bars and bubble gum.

Then he noticed his clothes were getting too big.

"My trousers are all stretching or something," said Treehorn to his mother. "I'm tripping on them all the time."

"That's too bad, dear," said his mother, looking into the oven. "I do hope this cake isn't going to fall," she said.

"And my sleeves come down way below my hands," said Treehorn. "So my shirts must be stretching, too."

"Think of that," said Treehorn's mother. "I just don't know why this cake isn't rising the way it should. Mrs. Abernale's cakes are *always* nice. They *always* rise."

Treehorn started out of the kitchen. He tripped on his trousers, which indeed did seem to be getting longer and longer.

At dinner that night Treehorn's father said, "Do sit up, Treehorn. I can hardly see your head."

"I *am* sitting up," said Treehorn. "This is as far up as I come. I think I must be shrinking or something."

"I'm sorry my cake didn't turn out very well," said Treehorn's mother.

"It's very nice, dear," said Treehorn's father politely.

By this time Treehorn could hardly see over the top of the table.

"Sit up, dear," said Treehorn's mother.

"I *am* sitting up," said Treehorn. "It's just that I'm shrinking."

"What, dear?" asked his mother.

"I'm shrinking. Getting smaller," said Treehorn.

"If you want to pretend you're shrinking, that's all right," said Treehorn's mother, "as long as you don't do it at the table."

"But I *am* shrinking," said Treehorn.

"Don't argue with your mother, Treehorn," said Treehorn's father.

"He does look a little smaller," said Treehorn's mother, looking at Treehorn. "Maybe he *is* shrinking."

"Nobody shrinks," said Treehorn's father.

"Well, I'm shrinking," said Treehorn. "Look at me."

Treehorn's father looked at Treehorn.

"Why, you're shrinking," said Treehorn's father. "Look, Emily, Treehorn is shrinking. He's much smaller than he used to be."

"Oh, dear," said Treehorn's mother. "First it was the cake, and now it's this. Everything happens at once."

"I *thought* I was shrinking," said Treehorn, and he went into the den to turn on the television set.

Treehorn liked to watch television. Now he lay on his stomach in front of the television set and watched one of his favorite programs. He had fifty-six favorite programs.

During the commercials, Treehorn always listened to his mother and father talking together, unless they were having a boring conversation. If they were having a boring conversation, he listened to the commercials.

Now he listened to his mother and father.

"He really is getting smaller," said Treehorn's mother. "What will we do? What will people say?"

"Why, they'll say he's getting smaller," said Treehorn's father. He thought for a moment. "I wonder if he's doing it on purpose. Just to be different."

"Why would he want to be different?" asked Treehorn's mother.

Treehorn started listening to the commercial.

The next morning Treehorn was still smaller. His regular clothes were much too big to wear. He rummaged around in his closet until he found some of his last year's clothes. They were much too big, too, but he put them on and rolled up the pants and rolled up the sleeves and went down to breakfast.

Treehorn liked cereal for breakfast. But mostly he liked cereal boxes. He always read every single thing on the cereal box while he was eating breakfast. And he always sent in for the things the cereal box said he could send for.

In a box in his closet Treehorn saved all of the things he had sent in for from cereal box tops. He had puzzles and special rings and flashlights and pictures of all of the presidents and pictures of all of the baseball players and he had pictures of scenes suitable for framing, which he had never framed because he didn't like them very much, and he had all kinds of games and pens and models.

Today on the cereal box was a very special offer of a very special whistle that only dogs could hear. Treehorn did not have a dog, but he thought it would be nice to have a whistle that dogs could hear, even if *he* couldn't hear it. Even if *dogs* couldn't hear it, it would be nice to have a whistle, just to have it.

He decided to eat all of the cereal in the box so he could send in this morning for the whistle. His mother never let him send in for anything until he had eaten all of the cereal in the box.

Treehorn filled in all of the blank spaces for his name and address and then he went to get his money out of the piggy bank on the kitchen counter, but he couldn't reach it.

"I certainly *am* getting smaller," thought Treehorn. He climbed up on a chair and got the piggy bank and shook out a dime.

His mother was cleaning the refrigerator. "You know how I hate to have you climb up on the chairs, dear," she said. She went into the living room to dust.

Treehorn put the piggy bank in the bottom kitchen drawer.

"That way I can get it no matter *how* little I get," he thought.

He found an envelope and put a stamp on it and put the dime and the box top in so he could mail the letter on the way to school. The mailbox was right next to the bus stop.

It was hard to walk to the bus stop because his shoes kept slipping off, but he got there in plenty of time, shuffling. He couldn't reach the mailbox slot to put the letter in, so he handed the letter to one of his friends, Moshie, and asked him to put it in. Moshie put it in. "How come you can't mail it yourself, stupid?" asked Moshie.

"Because I'm shrinking," explained Treehorn. "I'm shrinking and I'm too little to reach the mailbox."

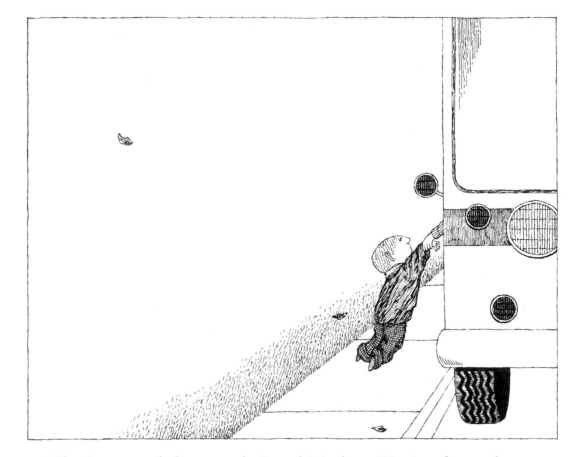

"That's a stupid thing to do," said Moshie. "You're *always* doing stupid things, but that's the *stupidest*."

When Treehorn tried to get on the school bus, everyone was pushing and shoving. The bus driver said, "All the way back in the bus, step all the way back." Then he saw Treehorn trying to climb onto the bus.

"Let that little kid on," said the bus driver.

Treehorn was helped onto the bus. The bus driver said, "You can stay right up here next to me if you want to, because you're so little."

"It's me, Treehorn," said Treehorn to his friend the bus driver.

The bus driver looked down at Treehorn. "You do look like Treehorn, at that," he said. "Only smaller. Treehorn isn't that little."

"I am Treehorn. I'm just getting smaller," said Treehorn.

"Nobody gets smaller," said the bus driver. "You must be Treehorn's kid brother. What's your name?"

"Treehorn," said Treehorn.

"First time I ever heard of a family naming two boys the same name," said the bus driver. "Guess they couldn't think of any other name, once they thought of Treehorn."

Treehorn said nothing.

When he went into class, his teacher said, "Nursery school is down at the end of the hall, honey."

"I'm Treehorn," said Treehorn.

"If you're Treehorn, why are you so small?" asked the teacher.

"Because I'm shrinking," said Treehorn. "I'm getting smaller."

"Well, I'll let it go for today," said his teacher. "But see that it's taken care of before tomorrow. We don't shrink in this class."

After recess, Treehorn was thirsty, so he went down the hall to the water bubbler. He couldn't reach it, and he tried to jump up high enough. He still couldn't get a drink, but he kept jumping up and down, trying.

His teacher walked by. "Why, Treehorn," she said. "That isn't like you, jumping up and down in the hall. Just because you're shrinking, it does not mean that you have special privileges. What if all the children in the *school* started jumping up and down in the halls? I'm afraid you'll have to go to the Principal's office, Treehorn."

So Treehorn went to the Principal's office.

"I'm supposed to see the Principal," said Treehorn to the lady in the Principal's outer office.

"It's a very busy day," said the lady. "Please check here on this form the reason you have to see him. That will save time. Be sure to put your name down, too. That will save time. And write clearly. That will save time."

Treehorn looked at the form:

CHECK REASON YOU HAVE TO
SEE PRINCIPAL (that will save time)

❑ 1. Talking in class
❑ 2. Chewing gum in class
❑ 3. Talking back to teacher
❑ 4. Unexcused absence
❑ 5. Unexcused illness
❑ 6. Unexcused behavior

P.T.O.

There were many things to check, but Treehorn couldn't find one that said "Being Too Small to Reach the Water Bubbler." He finally wrote in "SHRINKING."

When the lady said he could see the Principal, Treehorn went into the Principal's office with his form.

The Principal looked at the form, and then he looked at Treehorn. Then he looked at the form again.

"I can't read this," said the Principal. "It looks like SHIRKING. You're not SHIRK-ING, are you, Treehorn? We can't have any shirkers here, you know. We're a team, and we all have to do our very best."

"It says SHRINKING," said Treehorn. "I'm shrinking."

"Shrinking, eh?" said the Principal. "Well, now, I'm very sorry to hear that, Treehorn. You were right to come to me. That's what I'm here for. To guide. Not to punish, but to guide. To guide all the members of my team. To solve all their problems."

"But I don't have any problems," said Treehorn. "I'm just shrinking."

"Well, I want you to know I'm right here when you need me,

Treehorn," said the Principal, "and I'm glad I was here to help you. A team is only as good as its coach, eh?"

The Principal stood up. "Goodbye, Treehorn. If you have any more problems, come straight to me, and I'll help you again. A problem isn't a problem once it's solved, right?"

By the end of the day Treehorn was still smaller.

At the dinner table that night he sat on several cushions so he could be high enough to see over the top of the table.

"He's still shrinking," sniffed Treehorn's mother. "Heaven knows I've *tried* to be a good mother."

"Maybe we should call a doctor," said Treehorn's father.

"I did," said Treehorn's mother. "I called every doctor in the Yellow Pages. But no one knew anything about shrinking problems."

She sniffed again. "Maybe he'll just keep getting smaller and smaller until he disappears."

"No one disappears," said Treehorn's father positively.

"That's right, they don't," said Treehorn's mother more cheerfully. "But no one shrinks, either," she said after a moment. "Finish your carrots, Treehorn."

The next morning Treehorn was so small he had to jump out of bed. On the floor was a game he'd pushed under there and forgotten about. He walked under the bed to look at it.

It was one of the games he'd sent in for from a cereal box. He had started playing it a couple of days ago, but he hadn't had a chance to finish it because his mother had called him to come right downstairs that minute and have his breakfast or he'd be late for school.

The Shrinking of Treehorn   63

THE *BIG* GAME
FOR KIDS TO GROW ON
IT'S TREMENDOUS! IT'S DIFFERENT!
IT'S FUN! IT'S EASY! IT'S COLOSSAL!
PLAY IT WITH FRIENDS!
PLAY IT ALONE!
Complete with Spinner, Board, Pieces,
and—!
COMPLETE INSTRUCTIONS!

Treehorn looked at the cover of the box.

The game was called THE *BIG* GAME FOR KIDS TO GROW ON.

Treehorn sat under the bed to finish playing the game.

He always liked to finish things, even if they were boring. Even if he was watching a boring program on TV, he always watched it right to the end. Games were the same way. He'd finish this one now. Where had he left off? He remembered he'd just had to move his piece back seven spaces on the board when his mother had called him.

He was so small now that the only way he could move the spinner was by kicking it, so he kicked it. It stopped at number 4. That meant he could move his piece ahead four spaces on the board.

The only way he could move the piece forward now was by carrying it, so he carried it. It was pretty heavy. He walked along the board to the fourth space. It said CONGRATULATIONS, AND UP YOU GO: ADVANCE THIRTEEN SPACES.

Treehorn started to carry his piece forward the thirteen spaces, but the piece seemed to be getting smaller. Or else *he* was getting *bigger*. That was it, he *was* getting bigger, because the bottom of the bed was getting close to his head. He pulled the game out from under the bed to finish playing it.

He kept moving the piece for-ward, but he didn't have to carry it any longer. In fact, he seemed to be getting bigger and bigger with each space he landed in.

"Well, I don't want to get *too* big," thought Treehorn. So he moved the piece ahead slowly from

one space to the next, getting bigger with each space, until he was his own regular size again. Then he put the spinner and the pieces and the instructions and the board back in the box for THE *BIG GAME FOR KIDS TO GROW ON* and put it in his closet. If he ever wanted to get bigger or smaller he could play it again, even if it *was* a pretty boring game.

Treehorn went down to breakfast and started to read the new cereal box. It said you could send for a hundred balloons. His mother was cleaning the living room. She came into the kitchen to get a dust rag.

"Don't put your elbows on the table while you're eating, dear," she said.

"Look," said Treehorn. "I'm my own size now. My own regular size."

"That's nice, dear," said Treehorn's mother. "It's a very nice size, I'm sure, and if I were you I wouldn't shrink any-more. Be sure to tell your father when he comes home tonight. He'll be so pleased." She went back to the living room and started to dust and vacuum.

That night Treehorn was watching TV. As he reached over to change  channels, he noticed that his hand was bright green. He looked in the mirror that was hanging over the television set. His face was green. His ears were green. His hair was green. He was green all over.

Treehorn sighed. "I don't think I'll tell anyone," he thought to him-self. "If I don't say anything, they won't notice."

Treehorn's mother came in. "Do turn the volume down a little, dear," she said. "Your father and I are having the Smedleys over to play bridge. Do comb your hair before they come, won't you, dear," said his mother as she walked back to the kitchen.

VIRGIE GOES TO SCHOOL WITH US BOYS

written by Elizabeth Fitzgerald Howard
illustrated by E. B. Lewis

Set shortly after the Civil War, and passed down through the generations, this is based on a true story from the life of the author's grandfather, Cornelius "C.C." Fitzgerald.

Virgie was always begging to go to school with us boys.
All summer long she kept asking and asking.

"School's too far," Nelson said.
"School's too long," Will said.
"School's too hard," George said.
"And you too little," Val said.
"I'm big enough. Tell them, C.C.," Virgie said to me.

"Virgie," Val kept right on, "you scarcely big as a field mouse.
And school's seven miles from here! That's one long, long walk. . . ."
"And besides," Nelson added, "we have to live at school all week!
You couldn't do that. You'd be crying for Mama and all!"
"Nelson, you know I won't be crying for Mama." Virgie stamped
her foot.
"Well anyway," Nelson continued, "there's hardly any girls that go.
Girls don't need school."
"That's not so, Nelson," I said. "Girls need to read and write
and do 'rithmetic too. Just like us boys."

Now didn't I tell you about our school?
For two years us boys—that's George and Will and Nelson and Val and me,
C.C.—been schooling at a place started by some folks who love the Lord.

Quakers, they call themselves.

They opened a school for black people after Mr. Lincoln

declared us free like we ought to be.

And I was beginning to wonder,

What about Virgie?

She was free too.

Couldn't she go to school with us boys?

Summertime going by,
one week gone,
and then another
with Virgie asking and asking...

Virgie picking pole beans or weighing grain for Papa.
Virgie sewing quilt squares or stirring soap for Mama.
Virgie always asking,
"Papa, Mama, can I go too?
Can I go to school?"

"Virgie, you'd be all tuckered out just getting there," Will said.
"Raw Head and Bloody Bones might grab you in those
woods on the way!" Nelson said. "Eat up a little old girl."
But Virgie never blinked an eye. She kept right on asking.
Till one day in the fields, Papa said,
"Boys, Virgie, me and your ma been thinking.
All free people need learning—
Old folks, young folks... small girls, too.
Virgie, next school time you can go.
You can go to school with the boys."

Summer over.
Harvest in.
School time here!
Sunday night everything ready.
Clean pair of underdrawers for each of us.
Extra shirt too.
And food for the whole week long.
Everything ready, but Nelson was frowning.
"Virgie's too little," he said.

Monday morning early

Mama cooked us big bowls of cornmeal. She cooked eggs, too.

Papa led our prayers. Safe journey. Clear minds.

And thanks to the good Lord for our own school.

"Take care of Virgie," Papa said after prayer time.

"And take care of each other."

Giving orders, George took the lead.
"Not too fast. Stay in a line."
We passed by our barn and Papa's mill,
then cut through Mr. McKinney's field.
"Virgie, keep up now," Val said.
Past old Mr. Smith's farm,
'round Dickson's pond.
"Whoa, Virgie, careful there," Will said. "That's poison ivy."

Up one hill
and down another,
up and down,
down to the creek.

We took off our shoes, rolled up our pants legs,
and stepped real careful on the upping stones.
The cold water woke our hot tired feet.
Virgie held her skirt with one hand, her shoes and bucket with the other.
Then all of a sudden she was sliding and slipping.
"Watch out, Virgie!" I yelled, trying to grab her, but...

Splash! In the creek she went.
"Now she'll cry," Nelson grumbled. But she didn't.
Virgie was laughing! "It's a warm day," she said. "My skirt will dry."
Virgie's all right, I thought.

"Let's go!" said George.
"Hurry up!" said Will. "It's looking like rain!"

Just when we were coming to the woods.
It's thick and leafy in there...dark even when the sun's bright.

And it's too quiet, but that's not the worst part.
Raw Head and Bloody Bones!
Didn't I tell you about Raw Head and Bloody Bones?
Get you if you're not good, folks said.
Might get you anyway.
"Don't be scared, Virgie," I told her.
"I'm not scared," she said, but she held my hand tight.
Nobody talked. We just walked. Silent 'cept for twigs crackling.

Trees leaned over us. Shadows got darker.
A branch snatched ahold of my shirt, and my heart quit beating.
Then Virgie whispered, "Let's sing!"

"Just like a girl!" Nelson said.
But pretty soon he was singing too. "Go Down Moses" and "Oh Freedom"
and "Eyes Have Seen the Glory" and all the songs we could think of.
The walk went faster then. Seemed not so dark.
Soon we were out of the woods
and away from old Raw Head and Bloody Bones!

Across one field
and then another.
"Almost there, Virgie.
Almost to town."

We passed by the Inn and the Courthouse
and the churches and all the shops,
as we followed Main Street to the top of the hill.
"Do you see it, Virgie? Do you see it?"
We were almost shouting.

Big.
Red brick.
Long high windows and
a wide-open door.
Our very own school.
Mr. Warner the headmaster came out to greet us.

"Welcome, boys. George, William, Valentine, Nelson, Cornelius.
(That's me, C.C.) Glad to see you back. And who is this fine young
lady here? Your sister?"
"Yes sir, this is Virgie," George said. "Virgie, speak up to Mr. Warner."
"Good morning, sir," Virgie said.

"Virgie's pretty smart for a girl, Mr. Warner," Nelson said.
Nelson said that!

"Come look, Virgie," I said, pulling her inside with me.
"See all the desks? See the books?"
Virgie was staring,
staring at everything.

Especially the bookcase.

"So many books!" she said. She touched one softly with her hand.

"Someday I'll read all these books!"

Already Virgie was seeming bigger.

"When we go home on Friday, C.C.," she said,

"we'll tell Mama and Papa all we've learned.

That way might seem like they've been to school too.

Learning to be free,

Just like us."

SIDEWAYS STORIES FROM WAYSIDE SCHOOL

written by Louis Sachar

MRS. GORF

Mrs. Gorf had a long tongue and pointed ears. She was the meanest teacher in Wayside School. She taught the class on the thirtieth story.

"If you children are bad," she warned, "or if you answer a problem wrong, I'll wiggle my ears, stick out my tongue, and turn you into apples!" Mrs. Gorf didn't like children, but she loved apples.

Joe couldn't add. He couldn't even count. But he knew that if he answered a problem wrong, he would be turned into an apple. So he copied from John. He didn't like to cheat, but Mrs. Gorf had never taught him how to add.

One day Mrs. Gorf caught Joe copying John's paper. She wiggled her ears—first her right one, then her left—stuck out her tongue, and turned Joe into an apple. Then she turned John into an apple for letting Joe cheat.

"Hey, that isn't fair," said Todd. "John was only trying to help a friend."

Mrs. Gorf wiggled her ears—first her right one, then her left—stuck out her tongue, and turned Todd into an apple. "Does anybody else have an opinion?" she asked.

Nobody said a word.

Mrs. Gorf laughed and placed the three apples on her desk.

Stephen started to cry. He couldn't help it. He was scared.

"I do not allow crying in the classroom," said Mrs. Gorf. She wiggled her ears—first her right one, then her left—stuck out her tongue, and turned Stephen into an apple.

For the rest of the day, the children were absolutely quiet. And when they went home, they were too scared even to talk to their parents.

But Joe, John, Todd, and Stephen couldn't go home. Mrs. Gorf just left them on her desk. They were able to talk to each other, but they didn't have much to say.

Their parents were very worried. They didn't know where their children were. Nobody seemed to know.

The next day Kathy was late for school. As soon as she walked in, Mrs. Gorf turned her into an apple.

Paul sneezed during class. He was turned into an apple.

Nancy said, "God bless you!" when Paul sneezed. Mrs. Gorf wiggled her ears—first her right one, then her left—stuck out her tongue, and turned Nancy into an apple.

Terrence fell out of his chair. He was turned into an apple.

Maurecia tried to run away. She was halfway to the door as Mrs. Gorf's right ear began to wiggle. When she reached the door, Mrs. Gorf's left ear wiggled. Maurecia opened the door and had one foot outside when Mrs. Gorf stuck out her tongue. Maurecia became an apple.

Mrs. Gorf picked up the apple from the floor and put it on her desk with the others. Then a funny thing happened. Mrs. Gorf turned around and fell over a piece of chalk.

The three Erics laughed. They were turned into apples.

Mrs. Gorf had a dozen apples on her desk: Joe, John, Todd, Stephen, Kathy, Paul, Nancy, Terrence, Maurecia, and the three Erics—Eric Fry, Eric Bacon, and Eric Ovens.

Louis, the yard teacher, walked into the classroom. He had missed the children at recess. He had heard that Mrs. Gorf was a mean teacher. So he came up to investigate. He saw the twelve apples on Mrs. Gorf's desk.

"I must be wrong," he thought. "She must be a good teacher if so many children bring her apples." He walked back down to the playground.

The next day a dozen more children were turned into apples. Louis, the yard teacher, came back into the room. He saw twenty-four apples on Mrs. Gorf's desk. There were only three children left in the class. "She must be the best teacher in the world," he thought.

By the end of the week all of the children were apples. Mrs. Gorf was very happy. "Now I can go home," she said. "I don't have to teach anymore. I won't have to walk up thirty flights of stairs ever again."

"You're not going anywhere," shouted Todd. He jumped off the desk and bopped Mrs. Gorf on the nose. The rest of the apples followed. Mrs. Gorf fell on the floor. The apples jumped all over her.

"Stop," she shouted, "or I'll turn you into applesauce!"

But the apples didn't stop, and Mrs. Gorf could do nothing about it.

"Turn us back into children," Todd demanded.

Mrs. Gorf had no choice. She stuck out her tongue, wiggled her ears—this time her left one first, then her right—and turned the apples back into children.

"All right," said Maurecia, "let's go get Louis. He'll know what to do."

"No!" screamed Mrs. Gorf. "I'll turn you back into apples." She wiggled her ears—first her right one, then her left—and stuck out her tongue. But Jenny held up a mirror, and Mrs. Gorf turned herself into an apple.

The children didn't know what to do. They didn't have a teacher. Even though Mrs. Gorf was mean, they didn't think it was right to leave her as an apple. But none of them knew how to wiggle their ears.

Louis, the yard teacher, walked in. "Where's Mrs. Gorf?" he asked.

Nobody said a word.

"Boy, am I hungry," said Louis. "I don't think Mrs. Gorf would mind if I ate this apple. After all, she always has so many."

He picked up the apple, which was really Mrs. Gorf, shined it up on his shirt, and ate it.

THE ARABOOLIES OF LIBERTY STREET

written by Sam Swope
illustrated by Barry Root

Once there was a street called Liberty Street, and Liberty Street was lined with white houses that were so much alike it was difficult to tell one from another. This was just the way fat General Pinch and his skinny wife liked it.

The Pinches spied on their neighbors all day long. They had nothing better to do. They hated anything that looked like fun. They got upset when Joy hung upside down from a maple tree. They got angry when Katie crept around like a tiger. They got *furious* when Jack spun around until he felt dizzy. And whenever the Pinches got upset, or angry, or *furious*, the General would grab his bullhorn and shout "I'll call in the army!" and the fun would have to stop, right then and there.

When summer came, the Pinches ordered the children to stay inside.

The kids were miserable. So were their parents, but what could they do? Everyone was terrified of the General and his army, and orders were orders: the children had to stay inside.

It was a lonely time.

General and Mrs. Pinch smiled nasty smiles and stood proudly at their windows, keeping a sharp lookout for fresh trouble—tulips growing, robins building nests, that kind of thing. And whenever the Pinches saw anything they didn't like, the General would haul out his bullhorn. "I'll call in the army!" he'd holler.

Liberty Street was certainly clean and quiet—you had to give the Pinches credit for that. But you never heard any music or laughter there, or saw any toys or happy children. It was a sad place, and that made the Pinches very glad.

Then one day the Araboolies came to Liberty Street and moved in next door to the Pinches. They gave the General and his wife a lot to look at.

For one thing, there were dozens and dozens of them: children and moms and dads and aunts and uncles and grandparents and great-grandparents and great-great-great-grandparents. For another, the Araboolies had pets. They had anteaters and porcupines. Elephants, walruses and sloths. They even had a wok, a few popaloks and a wild barumpuss!

Mrs. Pinch sucked in both cheeks. "Disgusting!" she hissed.

"I'll call in the army!" boomed the General.

But that didn't bother the Araboolies. They didn't speak English. They didn't know *what* those Pinches were screaming about.

Now, the Araboolies came from an island far away where people are born with colorful skin. Strangely enough, however, the Araboolies

were never the same color from one day to the next. For example, one day Grandfather Araboolie might be orange, Auntie Araboolie blue, and Baby Araboolie pink. But Gramps could just as easily have woken up yellow, Auntie green, and Baby purple. You just never knew.

At night, the Araboolies glowed in the dark.

"Revolting!" squawked Mrs. Pinch, stomping her feet.

"I'll call in the army!" bellowed the General.

The first improvement the Araboolies made to their home was to paint it with red and white zigzags. They decorated it with flashing colored lights and hung toys from the trees. Then they drew jungle scenes on the sidewalks and poured sand on the grass and made sand creatures.

The Araboolies weren't the neatest people in the world, truth to tell, but they sure knew how to have fun. They put their furniture all over the yard and lived outside—they played outside, ate outside and watched TV outside. The Araboolies even *slept* outside, all cuddled up like puppies in the biggest bed you ever saw in your life. They snored like crazy!

The animals lived inside—in the shower, in the sink, under the stairs and in the chimney. They ran all over the place! What a racket they made!

"No noise!" screeched Mrs. Pinch, shaking her bony fists in the air.

And you can guess what the General hollered.

But no matter how much the Pinches screamed, the Araboolies didn't pay any attention. They were having too much fun.

General and Mrs. Pinch were miserable. All this happiness was making them sick. Things were getting out of control! Why, before they knew it *all* the children of Liberty Street were outside playing boolanoola ball!

"This has got to stop!" shrieked Mrs. Pinch, her eyes popping out of her head.

Just then, Joy clobbered the boolanoola ball. It went up and up and up until—oh, no!—it crashed through the Pinches' window and smashed into the General's stomach—pow!—and knocked him flat!

"Ouch!" roared the General.

The Pinches were out in a flash.

"This means war!" wailed Mrs. Pinch.

"I'll call in the army!" cried the General, and he whipped out his walkie-talkie. "Come in, army!" he thundered. "Attack Liberty Street at dawn!"

Then the Pinches stormed home and slammed the door—but not before their cat Naomi had escaped and gone to the Araboolies' house to live.

The Araboolies smiled and shrugged, but the rest of Liberty Street was in a panic. The army was coming! Doors were locked and blinds were pulled down tight. Everyone was terrified!

Everyone, that is, but Joy. "Those mean old Pinches," she thought. "When their army comes, they'll take away the Araboolies. Well, I won't let them! I won't!"

And so she thought and thought and thought until she had an idea.

She waited until night came. And then, when the parents of Liberty Street were asleep, Joy tiptoed outside and sneaked around Liberty

Street, waking the other children and telling them her plan. "What a neat idea!" they said.

Because there wasn't a moment to lose, they all got busy right away. But they had to be very quiet so their parents wouldn't wake up. The children crept down to their basements and up to their attics. They dug through closets and drawers. They gathered together toys and balloons and finger paints. They rounded up scissors and wrapping paper and they pulled out decorations from Christmas, Thanksgiving and Halloween. Then they went outside.

Some of the children colored the houses and pasted animal cut-outs in the windows. Others decorated the trees and painted the sidewalks. They put toys everywhere and dragged furniture outside. They worked all night long. The last thing they did was to paint one another's faces.

The Araboolies snored through it all.

It was almost dawn when they were finished. Liberty Street had never ever looked wilder or more colorful, and the children were very proud.

Before long, they heard the angry rumble of the army approaching. The ground shook. Soon there were guns and bombs and helicopters and thousands of soldiers marching past the colorful homes of Liberty Street.

Now, armies, of course, don't think. They only follow orders. And General Pinch's orders were very clear. "There's a house on Liberty Street that's different!" he roared from his window. "It's disgusting! Get rid of it! And get rid of the weirdos who live in it!"

And so, with those orders in mind, the soldiers marched up Liberty Street. But all they saw were brightly painted homes and colorful people. No house was different. No one was weird. The soldiers didn't know what to do.

But when they finally reached the end of Liberty Street—there it was! A different house, plain and white, with a fat angry man and a nasty skinny woman inside. "That's them!" shouted the army. "They're the weirdos!"

"Charge!" ordered the General.

And the army did just that. The soldiers surrounded the house and tied it up with ropes. "Not us, you idiots!" squealed Mrs. Pinch.

"I'll call in the army!" cried the General.

But the army was already there, following orders.

And so it was that the Pinches and their house were yanked from the ground and dragged far, far away, as the children cheered and the Araboolies waved good-bye. And the terrible Pinches were never seen on Liberty Street ever again.

The Araboolies of Liberty Street

NO ONE IS GOING TO NASHVILLE

written by Mavis Jukes
illustrated by Lloyd Bloom

It was six o'clock in the morning. Sonia checked her alligator lizard. He was out of termites and possibly in a bad mood. She decided to leave him alone. Nobody else was up except Ms. Mackey, the goose. She was standing on the back deck, talking to herself.

Sonia sat in the kitchen with her knees inside her nightgown. She peered out the window. The moon was still up above the rooftops. The houses were beginning to pale.

There was a dog on the stoop! He was eating radishes on the mat.

Sonia opened the door. "Hello, doggy!" she said. She knelt down. "You like radishes?"

He licked her face.

"Have you been in the garbage?"

He signaled to her with his ears.

"Stay!" said Sonia. She went back in the house and clattered in the pot cupboard.

"What time is it, Sonia?" her father called from the bedroom.

Sonia didn't answer because he had forgotten to call her "Dr. Ackley." She filled the bottom of the egg poacher with water and left it on the stoop, then went into the house and to the bedroom. "Dad," she said. "What do you think is a good name for a dog?"

He was trying to doze. "I'm closing my eyes and thinking," he lied.

Sonia waited. "You're sleeping!" she said.

He opened one eye. "Names for dogs. Let's see. Dog names. Ask Annette. She's the dog lover. What *time* is it?"

"About six-fifteen," said Annette. "I heard the train go by a few minutes ago." She rolled over.

Sonia went over to her stepmother's side of the bed. "Annette!" she said. "What name do you like for a dog?"

Annette propped herself up on her elbows. Her hair fell onto the sheets in beautiful reddish loops. "A dog name? My favorite? Maxine. Absolutely. I used to have a dog named Maxine. She ate cabbages." Annette collapsed on the pillow.

"Here, Maxine!" called Sonia.

"Oh no," said her father. He slid beneath the blankets. "I can't stand it! Not a dog at six o'clock in the morning!"

The dog padded through the door and into the bedroom.

"Maxine," said Sonia, "I want you to meet my father, Richard, and my Wicked Stepmother, Annette."

Annette got up. "That's not a Maxine," she reported, "that's a Max." She put on Richard's loafers and shuffled into the kitchen.

Richard got up and put on his pants. Sonia and Max watched him search for his shoes. Max's ears were moving so wildly they could have been conducting a symphony.

"Weird ears," said Richard. He went into the kitchen.

Ms. Mackey stared through the glass at his feet and started honking. He opened the door a couple of inches. *"Quiet!"* he whispered. "You're not even supposed to live inside the city limits!"

She puffed her feathers.

"Beat it!" said Richard. "Go eat some snails!"

Off she waddled.

Sonia came into the kitchen wearing white pants and a white shirt with DR. S. ACKLEY, D.V.M. printed on the pocket with a felt-tip pen. She took something from the refrigerator on a paper plate and left again.

"What are we going to do about Max?" said Annette.

"Send him packing," said Richard.

"Do you really think it's going to be that easy?" said Annette.

"Yes. Sonia knows I cannot stand dogs. Neither can her mother. We've been through this before. She accepts it."

Annette turned from Richard. "Well, don't be too sure," she said.

Richard went into the living room.

"Guess what," said Sonia. "Max ate all the meat loaf." She waved the paper plate at him.

"Great, I was planning to have that for lunch," said Richard dryly. "Dr. Ackley, may I have a word with you?"

Sonia sat on the couch and dragged Max up onto her lap. Annette stood in the doorway, looking on. Sonia carefully tore two slits in the paper plate. Richard watched, his hands clasped behind his back. His thumbs were circling each other.

"About this dog—" said Richard. He walked across the room.

"You're gorgeous," said Sonia to Max. She pushed each of Max's ears through a slit in the plate. "There!" she said. "Now you have a hat!"

Max licked her. She licked him back. Richard made an unpleasant face.

"That hat looks great!" said Annette. "Where's the camera?"

Richard began again. "I know you really like the dog, but he belongs somewhere."

"With me," said Sonia. "He's been abandoned. He came to me. He passed all the other houses. He's supposed to be mine." She pulled each ear out a little farther.

Richard turned and paced. "I don't like saying no," he said. "It's harder for me to say no than it is for other fathers because we only see each other on weekends."

Annette opened the closet to look for the camera.

"But," said Richard, "since we only see each other on weekends, I have more reasons to say no than other fathers." He put his hands in his pockets and jingled some change. "Number one: I don't like dogs and they don't like me." Richard pulled out a couple of coins and tossed them in the air. He caught them. "Number two: While you're at your mother's apartment, the dog becomes my responsibility."

Annette looked at him.

"And Annette's," he added. "Anyhow, since you're at your mother's house all week long, and I would have to walk the dog—"

"I could walk him," said Annette.

"—and feed him *and* pay the vet bills—" He dropped the coins into his pocket and glanced at Annette. "I feel that it's my decision." Richard looked at Sonia. "I'm the father. And I'm saying no."

Max jumped down. He shook off the hat and tore it up.

"You call me Dr. Ackley because you *know* I am planning to be a veterinarian," said Sonia, "yet you don't want me to have experience in the field by having pets."

"You're being unfair," said Richard. "I do let you have pets. Even though they abuse me. Have you forgotten this?" He displayed a small scar on the side of his finger.

"How could I forget that?" said Sonia. "Fangs bit you."

"Yes, Fangs the Killer Lizard bit me," said Richard.

"Do you remember *how* it happened?" said Sonia.

A smile crept across Annette's face. She sat down and opened the newspaper.

"I don't recall, exactly," said Richard. "And it's a painful memory. Let's not go through it."

"Well, *I* remember exactly what happened," said Sonia. "You said that you were so fast you once won a pie-eating contest, and that when you were a kid people used to call you Swifty."

Richard pretended to be bored with the story.

"And," continued Sonia, "you said you bet you could put a termite down in front of Fangs before he could snap it out of your fingers."

Richard folded his arms and looked at the ceiling.

"I said, 'I bet you can't,'" said Sonia. "Annette said, 'Don't try it.'"

Richard stared over at Annette, who was behind the newspaper trying not to laugh.

"And," said Sonia, "Fangs bit you."

"I know you're laughing, Annette," said Richard as she turned the page. "Is this my fault, too?" He pulled up his pant leg. "What do you see here?" he asked.

"A white leg with blue hairs," said Sonia.

"Wrong!" said Richard. "A bruise. Laugh it up, Annette, at my expense!"

Annette folded the newspaper. "You were teasing Ms. Mackey, and she bit you."

"Teasing Mrs. Mackey!" said Richard. "I was getting mud off my zoris!"

"Mizzzzzzzzz Mackey," said Sonia. "You were washing your feet in *her* pool, knowing she hates bare feet, and she bit you."

Richard threw up his hands. "*Her* pool. Now it's *her* pool. I built that for carp or goldfish!"

"*We* built that," said Annette.

"For whatever I wanted to put in it, and I chose a goose," said Sonia.

"No dog!" shouted Richard. He stalked into the kitchen, Annette and Sonia following him. "Send Weirdears home!" He crashed through the pot cupboard. "Where's the other half of the egg poacher?" He banged a griddle onto the stove. "No dog! Discussion closed!"

Sonia and Max went out on the stoop. They stood there a moment. Then Sonia bent down and gripped Max's nose with both hands. She looked into his eyes, frowning. "Go home!" said Sonia, knowing that he *was* home.

By the time breakfast was over and the dishes were done, Max had been sent away so many times by Richard that he moved off the stoop and into the hedge.

At noon, Richard called the pound. Sonia and Annette were listening.

Richard said, "You only keep strays for five days? *Then* what? You must be kidding! Good-bye."

Sonia took the telephone from him. She dialed her mother's number. "Hello, Mom?"

Annette left the room.

"Mom, can you and I keep a nice dog that Dad *hates* but I *love*?" Sonia glared at Richard and said to her mother, "Just a minute, someone's listening." She stepped into the closet

with the telephone and closed the door. "Well, it would only be until we could locate the owner." Silence. "I *know* there are no dogs allowed in the apartment house, but nobody needs to know but us!" Silence, then mumbling. Sonia came out of the closet. "I know you were listening, Dad!"

"I admit it," said Richard. "And I'll tell you what. You really just want to locate the owner? Nobody told me that. Fair enough! You write a description of the dog. We'll run an ad in the classified section. We'll keep the dog as long as the pound would. By next weekend, we'll know something."

"Thanks, Dad!" Sonia gave him a hug.

Richard felt pleased with himself. He broke into a song.

Sonia ran to the freezer and took out four hot dogs. Then off she raced to her room for a pencil and paper. "Oops!" she said. She darted back into the kitchen and grabbed a handful of Cheerios out of the box. She opened the sliding door and threw the Cheerios onto the deck for Ms. Mackey. Then she said, "Dad? Will you please feed Fangs?"

"All right," said Richard. "I can deal with the lizard. Where's my leather glove?"

Sonia ran out the door. "Max!" she said. "Here!" She was breathless. "Here!" She fed him the hot dogs, one at a time.

Then Sonia wrote the ad:

> *Found. Brown dog with a white background.*
> *Wearing paper hat. Misbehaves. Has radish*
> *breath. Answers to the name "Weirdears." Call*
> *555-7161.*

Sonia put the paper in her "DR. S. ACKLEY, D.V.M." pocket, and had a tumble with Max on the lawn. They spent the afternoon together, being pals. When it was time to go to her mother's house, Sonia hugged Max and told him: "I'll see you again, so I won't say good-bye."

Max wagged his tail in a circle.

Sonia went into the house and handed Richard the ad.

"Sonia!" said Richard.

"Dr. Ackley," said Sonia.

"This doesn't even sound like the same dog! Max isn't a 'brown dog with a white background.' He's a white dog with brown spots!"

"Same thing," said Sonia.

"Also, Max doesn't misbehave. He's very polite," said Richard.

"Then why don't you like him?" said Sonia.

Richard turned the paper over, took a pen from his shirt, and clicked it once. "Let's see."

Sonia read over his shoulder as he wrote:

> *Found. White dog with brown spots.*
> *Vicinity Railroad Hill. Male. No tags.*
> *Medium-sized. Strange ears.*
> *Call 555-7161, through May 3rd.*

"What does it mean, 'through May 3rd'?" she asked.

"After that," said Richard, "we're going to let someone adopt him."

Sonia fell into a swoon on the rug. "Us," she thought as she lay on the floor with her eyes shut.

"Now," said Richard. "Off you go to your mother's. We're already late."

As they were leaving, Annette picked up Max and waved his paw at Sonia. Sonia grinned.

"Ridiculous!" said Richard. He gave Annette a kiss. "Be right back!"

The week passed by slowly. Neither the newspaper ad nor calls to the pound and police station produced Max's owner. On Friday evening, Richard and Annette sat on the couch, waiting for Sonia to arrive. Max put his nose on Richard's knee.

Richard looked at Annette. "What does he want?" he asked.

"He's courting you," said Annette as Max licked Richard's hand.

"He's *tasting* me," said Richard. "He's thinking about sinking his teeth in my leg."

A horn beeped in the driveway. "Here she is now," Richard said. He went out on the stoop and waved.

"See you Sunday!" called Sonia's mother to Richard. She whizzed backward out of the driveway.

Sonia took the steps two at a time and ran past Richard. "Max!" she said. "I knew you'd be here!"

"Unfortunately," said Richard. "No owner."

"That's what I figured," said Sonia. "So"—she dug in her pack—"I wrote the ad"—she handed a note to Richard—"for Max to be adopted."

"Great!" said Richard. He felt relieved. "Then you *do* understand."

Neatly, in multicolored ink, and decorated with pictures of iris and geraniums, Sonia had written:

> *Free. We don't want him. A weird dog. Blotchy-colored. Has ear problems. Tears hats. Lives in hedges. Wags tail in a circle instead of back and forth. Call 555-7161.*

"Sonia!" said Richard.

She pointed to the name on her pocket.

"Dr. Ackley!" they both said at once.

"Nobody will want to adopt the dog if we say *this* in the paper."

"I know," said Sonia.

"Well, I also wrote one," said Richard. "I've already had it placed in tomorrow's paper." He opened his wallet and unfolded a piece of paper.

He read it aloud:

> *"Free to a good home. Beautiful, medium-sized*
> *male, Shepherd-mix. Snow white with gorgeous*
> *brown dots. A real storybook dog that will be*
> *an excellent companion. Would prefer country*
> *environment. Loves children. Sweet disposition.*
> *Obedient. Expressive ears. Call 555-7161."*

Sonia looked at Richard and said, "Don't call me Dr. Ackley anymore." She turned and stormed into the kitchen. She unbuttoned her shirt and balled it up. She stuffed it into a box under the sink that was filled with bottles for the recycling center.

Very late that night, Sonia woke up. She slipped from her bed and found Max in the living room. She searched for some cowboy music on the radio. She held Max in her arms.

Annette appeared in the doorway. "What are you two doing up?"

"It might be our last night," said Sonia. "We're dancing. He weighs a ton." She turned off the radio and put Max down. "What are you doing up?"

"Restless," said Annette. "I keep hearing the trains—listen!" She put her finger to her lips. She closed her eyes. A train was drawing closer through the darkness to the station. They heard the lonesome wail of the train whistle. "It must be midnight. The freight is coming in."

Max whined softly. Sonia and Annette knelt beside him.

"I knew Mom or Dad wouldn't let me keep him," began Sonia. "Neither one of them likes dogs."

Max pushed his nose into Sonia's hand. She smoothed his whiskers. Annette said nothing.

"And," continued Sonia, "animals are better off in the country. It's just that I really believed that Max could be mine."

Annette didn't speak.

The freight train clattered away into the night. The whistle sounded faint and lost. They listened until it was gone.

Max sat with his neck stretched way back and his nose pointed up while they scratched his throat. He looked like a stork.

"Max reminds me of Maxine," said Annette quietly.

"Really?" said Sonia. "What happened to Maxine?"

"Nobody knows for sure," said Annette. "She went off one day and didn't come back."

"Oh," said Sonia.

"We lived near the tracks—"

"Oh," said Sonia.

"My father was an engineer. One night he came home looking very sad." Annette's eyes were filling. "And my father told me—"

Sonia clutched Annette's hand. "Don't tell me. You don't have to say it."

"And my father told me that Maxine—"

Sonia hid her face in Max's neck.

"—that Maxine may have hopped a freight," said Annette, "and gone to Nashville to be a country western star."

Richard appeared in the doorway. "What's going on?" he said. "Who's going to Nashville?"

"No one!" said Annette. She stood up. "No one is going to Nashville!"

"Okay!" said Richard. "No one is going to Nashville!"

Max and Sonia got up.

Everybody went back to bed.

At nine o'clock the next morning the telephone rang. Sonia heard her father say, "Between East Railroad and Grant. About eight blocks west of the station. Come on over and see how you like him."

Richard hung up the phone. "They're coming this morning."

Sonia said nothing.

"I don't expect to be here," said Annette. "I have errands to do."

An hour later a pickup pulled into the driveway. Max barked. A woman got out of the truck and stretched. A man wearing green cowboy boots got out, too, carrying a little girl wearing a felt jacket with cactuses on it and a red ballet skirt. She was holding an Eskimo Pie.

Richard walked down the steps with Max beside him. Sonia lingered in the doorway. Annette came out on the stoop, holding the box for the recycling center. Sonia's shirt was tucked between the bottles. Annette rested a corner of the box on the rail.

"Is this the dog?" said the woman. "He's a beauty!"

"Yes," said Richard.

The cowboy knelt down with his daughter. "Hey, partner!"

Max went over to them.

"Howdy, boy!"

The little girl put out her hand, and Max licked it.

"Do you have a yard?" asked Richard.

"A ranch," said the cowboy. "With a lake." He patted Max. "What's your name, boy?"

"Max," said Richard.

"Why, you doggone pelican!" the cowboy told Max. "I have an uncle named Max!"

"We'll take him," said the woman. "For our little girl."

Sonia came out on the stoop. "Annette! Could you ask them about taking a goose, too?" She was blinking back tears. "And an alligator lizard?"

Annette heard a whistle. The train was coming in. "Listen!" she said. "No one is going to Nashville!" She pulled Sonia's shirt from the box. The box fell from her arms and the bottles shattered on the cement.

"We're keeping the dog," said Annette. She almost choked on the words. She pressed the shirt into Sonia's hands.

Annette started down the steps. "We're keeping the dog!"

"Watch out for the glass!" said Richard.

Annette went to the little girl. "I'm sorry," she said. She picked up Max. She looked at Richard. "We're keeping this dog for our little girl." Tears were falling. She climbed the stairs.

"Okay! Okay! Watch out for the glass," said Richard.

Sonia was waiting. Annette put Max into her arms. "For Dr. Ackley," said Annette, "from your Wicked Stepmother and from your father, with love. Discussion closed."

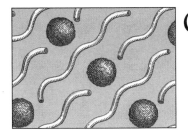

CLOUDY WITH A CHANCE OF MEATBALLS

written by Judi Barrett
illustrated by Ron Barrett

We were all sitting around the big kitchen table. It was Saturday morning. Pancake morning. Mom was squeezing oranges for juice. Henry and I were betting on how many pancakes we each could eat. And Grandpa was doing the flipping.

Seconds later, something flew through the air, headed toward the kitchen ceiling, and landed right on Henry.

After we realized that the flying object was only a pancake, we all laughed, even Grandpa. Breakfast continued quite uneventfully. All the other pancakes landed in the pan. And all of them were eaten, even the one that landed on Henry.

That night, touched off by the pancake incident at breakfast, Grandpa told us the best tall-tale bedtime story he'd ever told.

"Across an ocean, over lots of huge bumpy mountains, across three hot deserts and one smaller ocean, there lay the tiny town of Chewandswallow.

In most ways, it was very much like any other tiny town. It had a Main Street lined with stores, houses with trees and gardens around them, a schoolhouse, about three hundred people, and some assorted cats and dogs.

But there were no food stores in the town of Chewandswallow. They didn't need any. The sky supplied all the food they could possibly want.

The only thing that was really different about Chewandswallow was its weather. It came three times a day, at breakfast, lunch, and dinner. Everything that everyone ate came from the sky.

Whatever the weather served, that was what they ate.

But it never rained rain. It never snowed snow. And it never blew just wind. It rained things like soup and juice. It snowed mashed potatoes and green peas. And sometimes the wind blew in storms of hamburgers.

The people could watch the weather report on television in the morning and they would even hear a prediction for the next day's food.

When the townspeople went outside, they carried their plates, cups, glasses, forks, spoons, knives, and napkins with them. That way they would always be prepared for any kind of weather.

If there were leftovers, and there usually were, the people took them home and put them in their refrigerators in case they got hungry between meals.

The menu varied.

By the time they woke up in the morning, breakfast was coming down.

After a brief shower of orange juice, low clouds of sunny-side up eggs moved in, followed by pieces of toast. Butter and jelly sprinkled down for the toast. And most of the time it rained milk afterward.

Cloudy with a Chance of Meatballs   99

For lunch one day, frankfurters, already in their rolls, blew in from the northwest at about five miles an hour.

There were mustard clouds nearby. Then the wind shifted to the east and brought in baked beans.

A drizzle of soda finished off the meal.

Dinner one night consisted of lamb chops, becoming heavy at times, with occasional ketchup. Periods of peas and baked potatoes were followed by gradual clearing, with a wonderful Jell-O setting in the west.

The Sanitation Department of Chewandswallow had a rather un-
usual job for a sanitation department. It had to remove the food that fell
on the houses and sidewalks and lawns. The workers cleaned things up
after every meal and fed all the dogs and cats. Then they emptied some
of it into the surrounding oceans for the fish and turtles and whales to
eat. The rest of the food was put back into the earth so that the soil
would be richer for the people's flower gardens.

Life for the townspeople was delicious until the weather took a turn
for the worse.

One day there was nothing but Gorgonzola cheese all day long.

The next day there was only broccoli, all overcooked.

And the next day there were brussels sprouts and peanut butter with
mayonnaise.

Another day there was a pea soup fog. No one could see where they
were going, and they could barely find the rest of the meal that got stuck
in the fog.

The food was getting larger and larger, and so were the portions. The people were getting frightened. Violent storms blew up frequently. Awful things were happening.

One Tuesday there was a hurricane of bread and rolls all day long and into the night. There were soft rolls and hard rolls, some with seeds and some without. There was white bread and rye and whole wheat toast. Most of it was larger than they had ever seen bread and rolls before. It was a terrible day. Everyone had to stay indoors. Roofs were damaged, and the Sanitation Department was beside itself. The mess took the workers four days to clean up, and the sea was full of floating rolls.

To help out, the people piled up as much bread as they could in their backyards. The birds picked at it a bit, but it just stayed there and got staler and staler.

There was a storm of pancakes one morning and a downpour of maple syrup that nearly flooded the town. A huge pancake covered the school. No one could get it off because of its weight, so they had to close the school.

Lunch one day brought fifteen-inch drifts of cream cheese and jelly sandwiches. Everyone ate themselves sick and the day ended with a stomachache.

There was an awful salt-and-pepper wind accompanied by an even worse tomato tornado. People were sneezing themselves silly and running to avoid the tomatoes. The town was a mess. There were seeds and pulp everywhere.

The Sanitation Department gave up. The job was too big.

Everyone feared for their lives. They couldn't go outside most of the time. Many houses had been badly damaged by giant meatballs, stores were boarded up, and there was no more school for the children.

So a decision was made to abandon the town of Chewandswallow.

It was a matter of survival.

Cloudy with a Chance of Meatballs

The people glued together the giant pieces of stale bread sandwich-style with peanut butter, took the absolute necessities with them, and set sail on their rafts for a new land.

After being afloat for a week, they finally reached a small coastal town, which welcomed them. The bread had held up surprisingly well, well enough for them to build temporary houses for themselves out of it.

The children began school again, and the adults all tried to find places for themselves in the new land. The biggest change they had to make was getting used to buying food at a supermarket. They found it odd that the food was kept on shelves, packaged in boxes, cans, and bottles. Meat that had to be cooked was kept in large refrigerators. Nothing came down from the sky except rain and snow. The clouds above their heads were not made of fried eggs. No one ever got hit by a hamburger again.

And nobody dared to go back to Chewandswallow to find out what had happened to it. They were too afraid."

Henry and I were awake until the very end of Grandpa's story. I remember his good-night kiss.

The next morning we woke up to see snow falling outside our window.

We ran downstairs for breakfast and ate it a little faster than usual so we could go sledding with Grandpa.

It's funny, but even as we were sliding down the hill we thought we saw a giant pat of butter at the top, and we could almost smell mashed potatoes.

WILMA UNLIMITED

written by Kathleen Krull
illustrated by David Diaz

This is the true story of a young woman who overcame the
crippling disease of polio to become the world's fastest runner.

No one expected such a tiny girl to have a first birthday. In Clarksville, Tennessee, in 1940, life for a baby who weighed just over four pounds at birth was sure to be limited.

But most babies didn't have nineteen older brothers and sisters to watch over them. Most babies didn't have a mother who knew home remedies and a father who worked several jobs.

Most babies weren't Wilma Rudolph.

Wilma did celebrate her first birthday, and everyone noticed that as soon as this girl could walk, she ran or jumped instead.

She worried people, though—she was always so small and sickly. If a brother or sister had a cold, she got double pneumonia. If one of them had measles, Wilma got measles, too, plus mumps and chicken pox.

Her mother always nursed her at home. Doctors were a luxury for the Rudolph family, and anyway, only one doctor in Clarksville would treat black people.

Just before Wilma turned five, she got sicker than ever. Her sisters and brothers heaped all the family's blankets on her, trying to keep her warm.

During that sickness, Wilma's left leg twisted inward, and she couldn't move it back. Not even Wilma's mother knew what was wrong.

The doctor came to see her then. Besides scarlet fever, he said, Wilma had also been stricken with polio. In those days, most children who got polio either died or were permanently crippled. There was no cure.

The news spread around Clarksville. Wilma, that lively girl, would never walk again.

But Wilma kept moving any way she could. By hopping on one foot, she could get herself around the house, to the outhouse in the backyard, and even, on Sundays, to church.

Wilma's mother urged her on. Mrs. Rudolph had plenty to do—cooking, cleaning, sewing patterned flour sacks into clothes for her children, now twenty-two in all. Yet twice every week, she and Wilma took the bus to the nearest hospital that would treat black patients, some fifty miles away in Nashville. They rode together in the back, the only place blacks were allowed to sit.

Doctors and nurses at the hospital helped Wilma do exercises to make her paralyzed leg stronger. At home, Wilma practiced them constantly, even when it hurt.

To Wilma, what hurt most was that the local school wouldn't let her

attend because she couldn't walk. Tearful and lonely, she watched her brothers and sisters run off to school each day, leaving her behind. Finally, tired of crying all the time, she decided she had to fight back—somehow.

Wilma worked so hard at her exercises that the doctors decided she was ready for a heavy steel brace. With the brace supporting her leg, she didn't have to hop anymore. School was possible at last.

But it wasn't the happy place she had imagined. Her classmates made fun of her brace. During playground games she could only sit on the sidelines, twitchy with impatience. She studied the other kids for hours—memorizing moves, watching the ball zoom through the rim of the bushel basket they used as a hoop.

Wilma fought the sadness by doing more leg exercises. Her family always cheered her on, and Wilma did everything she could to keep them from worrying about her. At times her leg really did seem to be getting stronger. Other times it just hurt.

One Sunday, on her way to church, Wilma felt especially good. She and her family had always found strength in their faith, and church was Wilma's favorite place in the world. Everyone she knew would be there—talking and laughing, praying and singing. It would be just the place to try the bravest thing she had ever done.

She hung back while people filled the old building. Standing alone, the sound of hymns coloring the air, she unbuckled her heavy brace and

set it by the church's front door. Taking a deep breath, she moved one foot in front of the other, her knees trembling violently. She took her mind off her knees by concentrating on taking another breath, and then another.

Whispers rippled throughout the gathering: Wilma Rudolph was *walking*. Row by row, heads turned toward her as she walked alone down the aisle. Her large family, all her family's friends, everyone from school—each person stared wide-eyed. The singing never stopped; it seemed to burst right through the walls and into the trees. Finally, Wilma reached a seat in the front and began singing too, her smile triumphant.

Wilma practiced walking as often as she could after that, and when she was twelve years old, she was able to take off the brace for good. She and her mother realized she could get along without it, so one memorable day, they wrapped the hated brace in a box and mailed it back to the hospital.

As soon as Wilma sent that box away, she knew her life was beginning all over again.

After years of sitting on the sidelines, Wilma couldn't wait to throw herself into basketball, the game she had most liked to watch. She was skinny but no longer tiny. Her long, long legs would propel her across the court and through the air, and she knew all the rules and all the moves.

In high school, she led her basketball team to one victory after another. Eventually, she took the team all the way to the Tennessee state championships. There, to everyone's astonishment, her team lost.

Wilma had become accustomed to winning. Now she slumped on the bench, all the liveliness knocked out of her.

But at the game that day was a college coach. He admired Wilma's basketball playing but was especially impressed by the way she ran. He wanted her for his track-and-field team.

With his help, Wilma won a full athletic scholarship to Tennessee State University. She was the first member of her family to go to college.

Eight years after she mailed her brace away, Wilma's long legs and years of hard work carried her thousands of miles from Clarksville, Tennessee. The summer of 1960 she arrived in Rome, Italy, to represent the United States at the Olympic Games—as a runner.

Just participating in the Olympics was a deeply personal victory for Wilma, but her chances of winning a race were limited. Simply walking in Rome's shimmering heat was a chore, and athletes from other countries had run faster races than Wilma ever had. Women weren't thought to run very well, anyway; track-and-field was considered a sport for men.

And the pressure from the public was intense—for the first time ever, the Olympics would be shown on television, and all the athletes knew that more than one hundred million people would be watching. Worst of all, Wilma had twisted her ankle just after she arrived in Rome. It was still swollen and painful on the day of her first race.

Yet once it was her turn to compete, Wilma forgot her ankle and everything else. She lunged forward, not thinking about her fear, her pain, or the sweat flying off her face. She ran better than she ever had before. And she ran better than anyone else.

Grabbing the attention of the whole world, Wilma Rudolph of the United States won the 100-meter dash. No one else even came close. An Olympic gold medal was hers to take home.

So when it was time for the 200-meter dash, Wilma's graceful long legs were already famous. Her ears buzzed with the sound of the crowd chanting her name. Such support helped her ignore the rain that was beginning to fall. At the crack of the starting gun, she surged into the humid air like a tornado. When she crossed the finish line, she had done it again. She finished far ahead of everyone else. She had earned her second gold medal. Wet and breathless, Wilma was exhilarated by the double triumph. The crowd went wild.

The 400-meter relay race was yet to come. Wilma's team faced the toughest competition of all. And as the fourth and final runner on her team, it was Wilma who had to cross the finish line.

Wilma's teammates ran well, passed the baton smoothly, and kept the team in first place. Wilma readied herself for the dash to the finish line as her third teammate ran toward her. She reached back for the baton— and nearly dropped it. As she tried to recover from the fumble, two other runners sped past her. Wilma and her team were suddenly in third place.

Ever since the day she had walked down the aisle at church, Wilma had known the power of concentration. Now, legs pumping, she put her mind to work. In a final, electrifying burst of speed, she pulled ahead. By a fraction of a second, she was the first to blast across the finish line. The thundering cheers matched the thundering of her own heart. She had made history. She had won for an astounding third time.

At her third ceremony that week, as the band played "The Star-Spangled Banner," Wilma stood tall and still, like a queen, the last of her three Olympic gold medals hanging around her neck.

Wilma Rudolph, once known as the sickliest child in Clarksville, had become the fastest woman in the world.

CATWINGS

written by Ursula K. Le Guin
illustrated by S. D. Schindler

CHAPTER 1

MRS. JANE TABBY could not explain why all four of her children had wings.

"I suppose their father was a fly-by-night," a neighbor said, and laughed unpleasantly, sneaking round the dumpster.

"Maybe they have wings because I dreamed, before they were born, that I could fly away from this neighborhood," said Mrs. Jane Tabby. "Thelma, your face is dirty; wash it. Roger, stop hitting James. Harriet, when you purr, you should close your eyes partway and knead me with your front paws; yes, that's the way. How is the milk this morning, children?"

"It's very good, Mother, thank you," they answered happily. They were beautiful children, well brought up. But Mrs. Tabby worried about them secretly. It really was a terrible neighborhood, and getting worse. Car wheels and truck wheels rolling past all day—rubbish and litter—hungry dogs—endless shoes and boots walking, running, stamping, kicking—nowhere safe and quiet, and less and less to eat. Most of the sparrows had moved away. The rats were fierce and dangerous; the mice were shy and scrawny.

So the children's wings were the least of Mrs. Tabby's worries. She washed those silky wings every day, along with chins and paws and tails,

and wondered about them now and then, but she worked too hard finding food and bringing up the family to think much about things she didn't understand.

But when the huge dog chased little Harriet and cornered her behind the garbage can, lunging at her with open, white-toothed jaws, and Harriet with one desperate mew flew straight up into the air and over the dog's staring head and lighted on a rooftop—then Mrs. Tabby understood.

The dog went off growling, its tail between its legs.

"Come down now, Harriet," her mother called. "Children, come here please, all of you."

They all came back to the dumpster. Harriet was still trembling. The others all purred with her till she was calm, and then Mrs. Jane Tabby said: "Children, I dreamed a dream before you were born, and I see now what it meant. This is not a good place to grow up in, and you have wings to fly from it. I want you to do that. I know you've been practic-ing. I saw James flying across the alley last night—and yes, I saw you doing nosedives, too, Roger. I think you are ready. I want you to have a good dinner and fly away—far away."

"But Mother—" said Thelma, and burst into tears.

"I have no wish to leave," said Mrs. Tabby quietly. "My work is here. Mr. Tom Jones pro-posed to me last night, and I intend to accept him. I don't want you children underfoot!"

All the children wept, but they knew that that is the way it must be, in cat fami-lies. They were proud, too, that their mother trusted them to look after themselves. So all together they had a good dinner from the garbage can that the dog had knocked over. Then Thelma, Roger, James, and Harriet purred good-bye to their dear mother, and one after another they spread their wings and flew up, over the alley, over the roofs, away.

Mrs. Jane Tabby watched them. Her heart was full of fear and pride.

"They are remarkable children, Jane," said Mr. Tom Jones in his soft, deep voice.

"Ours will be remarkable too, Tom," said Mrs. Tabby.

CHAPTER 2

As THELMA, Roger, James, and Harriet flew on, all they could see beneath them, mile after mile, was the city's roofs, the city's streets.

A pigeon came swooping up to join them. It flew along with them, peering at them uneasily from its little, round, red eye. "What kind of birds are you, anyways?" it finally asked.

"Passenger pigeons," James said promptly.

Harriet mewed with laughter.

The pigeon jumped in mid-air, stared at her, and then turned and swooped away from them in a great, quick curve.

"I wish I could fly like that," said Roger.

"Pigeons are really dumb," James muttered.

"But my wings ache already," Roger said, and Thelma said, "So do mine. Let's land somewhere and rest."

Little Harriet was already heading down towards a church steeple.

They clung to the carvings on the church roof and got a drink of water from the roof gutters.

"Sitting in the catbird seat!" sang Harriet, perched on a pinnacle.

"It looks different over there," said Thelma, pointing her nose to the west. "It looks softer."

They all gazed earnestly westward, but cats don't see the distance clearly.

"Well, if it's different, let's try it," said James, and they set off again. They could not fly with untiring ease, like the pigeons. Mrs. Tabby had always seen to it that they ate well, and so they were quite plump, and had to beat their wings hard to keep their weight aloft. They learned how to glide, not beating their wings, letting the wind bear them up; but Harriet found gliding difficult, and wobbled badly.

After another hour or so they landed on the roof of a huge factory, even though the air there smelled terrible, and there they slept for a

while in a weary, furry heap. Then, towards nightfall, very hungry—for nothing gives an appetite like flying—they woke and flew on.

The sun set. The city lights came on, long strings and chains of lights below them, stretching out towards darkness. Towards darkness they flew, and at last, when around them and under them everything was dark except for one light twinkling over the hill, they descended slowly from the air and landed on the ground.

A soft ground—a strange ground! The only ground they knew was pavement, asphalt, cement. This was all new to them, dirt, earth, dead leaves, grass, twigs, mushrooms, worms. It all smelled extremely interesting. A little creek ran nearby. They heard the song of it and went to drink, for they were very thirsty. After drinking, Roger stayed crouching on the bank, his nose in the water, his eyes gazing.

"What's that in the water?" he whispered.

The others came and gazed. They could just make out something moving in the water, in the starlight—a silvery flicker, a gleam. Roger's paw shot out . . .

"I think it's dinner," he said.

After dinner, they curled up together again under a bush and fell asleep. But first Thelma, then Roger, then James, and then small Harriet would lift their head, open an eye, listen a moment, on guard. They knew they had come to a much better place than the alley, but they also knew that every place is dangerous, whether you are a fish, or a cat, or even a cat with wings.

CHAPTER 3

"It's ABSOLUTELY unfair," the thrush cried.

"Unjust!" the finch agreed.

"Intolerable!" yelled the blue jay.

"I don't see why," a mouse said. "You've always had wings. Now they do. What's unfair about that?"

The fish in the creek said nothing. Fish never do. Few people know what fish think about injustice, or anything else.

"I was bringing a twig to the nest just this morning, and a *cat* flew down, a cat *flew* down, from the top of the Home Oak, and *grinned* at me in mid-air!" the thrush said, and all the other songbirds cried, "Shocking! Unheard of! Not allowed!"

"You could try tunnels," said the mouse, and trotted off.

The birds had to learn to get along with the Flying Tabbies. Most of the birds, in fact, were more frightened and outraged than really endangered, since they were far better fliers than Roger, Thelma, Harriet, and James. The birds never got their wings tangled up in pine branches and never absent-mindedly bumped into tree trunks, and when pursued they could escape by speeding up or taking evasive action. But they were alarmed, and with good cause, about their fledglings. Many birds had eggs in the nest now; when the babies hatched, how could they be kept safe from a cat who could fly up and perch on the slenderest branch, among the thickest leaves?

It took a while for the Owl to understand this. Owl is not a quick thinker. She is a long thinker. It was late in spring, one evening, when she was gazing fondly at her two new owlets, that she saw James flitting by, chasing bats. And she slowly thought, "This will not do . . ."

And softly Owl spread her great gray wings, and silently flew after James, her talons opening.

THE FLYING TABBIES had made their nest in a hole halfway up a big elm, above fox and coyote level and too small for raccoons to get into. Thelma and Harriet were washing each other's necks and talking over the day's adventures when they heard a pitiful crying at the foot of the tree.

"James!" cried Harriet.

He was crouching under the bushes, all scratched and bleeding, and one of his wings dragged upon the ground.

"It was the Owl," he said, when his sisters had helped him climb painfully up the tree trunk to their home hole. "I just escaped. She caught me, but I scratched her, and she let go for a moment."

And just then Roger came scrambling into the nest with his eyes round and black and full of fear. "She's after me!" he cried. "The Owl!"

They all washed James's wounds till he fell asleep.

"Now we know how the little birds feel," said Thelma grimly.

"What will James do?" Harriet whispered. "Will he ever fly again?"

"He'd better not," said a soft, large voice just outside their door. The Owl was sitting there.

The Tabbies looked at one another. They did not say a word till morning came.

At sunrise Thelma peered cautiously out. The Owl was gone. "Until this evening," said Thelma.

From then on they had to hunt in the daytime and hide in their nest all night; for the Owl thinks slowly, but the Owl thinks long.

James was ill for days and could not hunt at all. When he recovered, he was very thin and could not fly much, for his left wing soon grew stiff and lame. He never complained. He sat for hours by the creek, his wings folded, fishing. The fish did not complain either. They never do.

One night of early summer the Tabbies were all curled in their home hole, rather tired and discouraged. A raccoon family was quarreling loudly in the next tree. Thelma had found nothing to eat all day but a shrew, which gave her indigestion. A coyote had chased Roger away from the wood rat he had been about to catch that afternoon. James's fishing had been unsuccessful. The Owl kept flying past on silent wings, saying nothing.

Two young male raccoons in the next tree started a fight, cursing and shouting insults. The other raccoons all joined in, screeching and scratching and swearing.

"It sounds just like the old alley," James remarked.

"Do you remember the Shoes?" Harriet asked dreamily. She was looking quite plump, perhaps because she was so small. Her sister and brothers had become thin and rather scruffy.

"Yes," James said. "Some of them chased me once."

"Do you remember the Hands?" Roger asked.

"Yes," Thelma said. "Some of them picked me up once. When I was just a kitten."

"What did they do—the Hands?" Harriet asked.

"They squeezed me. It hurt. And the hands person was shouting—'Wings! Wings! It has wings!'—that's what it kept shouting in its silly voice. And squeezing me."

"What did you do?"

"I bit it," Thelma said, with modest pride. "I bit it, and it dropped me, and I ran back to Mother, under the dumpster. I didn't know how to fly yet."

"I saw one today," said Harriet.

"What? A Hands? A Shoes?" said Thelma.

"A human bean?" said James.

"A human being?" Roger said.

"Yes," said Harriet. "It saw me, too."

"Did it chase you?"

"Did it kick you?"

"Did it throw things at you?"

"No. It just stood and watched me flying. And its eyes got round, just like ours."

"Mother always said," Thelma remarked thoughtfully, "that if you found the right kind of Hands, you'd never have to hunt again. But if you found the wrong kind, it would be worse than dogs, she said."

"I think this one is the right kind," said Harriet.

"What makes you think so?" Roger asked, sounding like their mother.

"Because it ran off and came back with a plate full of dinner," Harriet said. "And it put the dinner down on that big stump at the edge of the field where we scared the cows that day, you know. And then it went off quite a way, and sat down, and just watched me. So I flew over and ate

the dinner. It was an interesting dinner. Like what we used to get in the alley, but fresher. And," said Harriet, sounding like their mother, "I'm going back there tomorrow and see what's on that stump."

"You just be careful, Harriet Tabby!" said Thelma, sounding even more like their mother.

CHAPTER 4

THE NEXT DAY, when Harriet went to the big stump at the edge of the cow pasture, flying low and cautiously, she found a tin pie-plate of meat scraps and kibbled catfood waiting for her. The girl from Overhill Farm was also waiting for her, sitting about twenty feet away from the stump and holding very still. Susan Brown was her name, and she was eight years old. She watched Harriet fly out of the woods and hover like a fat hummingbird over the stump, then settle down, fold her wings neatly, and eat. Susan Brown held her breath. Her eyes grew round.

The next day, when Harriet and Roger flew cautiously out of the woods and hovered over the stump, Susan was sitting about fifteen feet away, and beside her sat her twelve-year-old brother Hank. He had not believed a word she said about flying cats. Now his eyes were perfectly round, and he was holding his breath.

Harriet and Roger settled down to eat.

"You didn't say there were two of them," Hank whispered to his sister.

Harriet and Roger sat on the stump licking their whiskers clean.

"You didn't say there were two of them," Roger whispered to his sister.

"I didn't know!" both the sisters whispered back. "There was only one, yesterday. But they look nice—don't they?"

THE NEXT DAY, Hank and Susan put out two pie-tins of cat dinner on the stump, then went ten steps away, sat down in the grass, and waited.

Harriet flew boldly from the woods and alighted on the stump.

Roger followed her. Then—"Oh, look!" Susan whispered—came Thelma, flying very slowly, with a disapproving expression on her face. And finally—"Oh, look, *look!*" Susan whispered—James, flying low and lame, flapped over to the stump, landed on it, and began to eat. He ate, and ate, and ate. He even growled once at Thelma, who moved over to the other pie-tin.

The two children watched the four winged cats.

Harriet, quite full, washed her face, and watched the children.

Thelma finished a last tasty kibble, washed her left front paw, and gazed at the children. Suddenly she flew up from the stump and straight at them. They ducked as she went over. She flew right round both their heads and then back to the stump.

"Testing," she said to Harriet, James, and Roger.

"If she does it again, don't catch her," Hank said to Susan. "It'd scare her off."

"You think I'm *stupid?*" Susan hissed.

They sat still. The cats sat still. Cows ate grass nearby. The sun shone.

"Kitty," Susan said in a soft, high voice. "Kitty kit-kit-kit-kit-kit-cat, kitty-cat, kitty-wings, kittywings, catwings!"

Harriet jumped off the stump into the air, performed a cartwheel, and flew loop-the-loop over to Susan. She landed on Susan's shoulder and sat there, holding on tight and purring in Susan's ear.

"I will never never never ever catch you, or cage you, or do anything to you you don't want me to do," Susan said to Harriet. "I promise. Hank, you promise too."

"Purr," said Harriet.

"I promise. And we'll never ever tell anybody else," Hank said, rather fiercely. "Ever! Because—you know how people are. If people saw them—"

"I promise," Susan said. She and Hank shook hands, promising.

Roger flew gracefully over and landed on Hank's shoulder.

"Purr," said Roger.

"They could live in the old barn," Susan said. "Nobody ever goes there but us. There's that dovecote up in the loft, with all those holes in the wall where the doves flew in and out."

"We can take hay up there and make them a place to sleep," Hank said.

"Purr," said Roger.

Very softly and gently Hank raised his hand and stroked Roger right between the wings.

"Oooh," said James, watching. He jumped down off the stump and came trotting over to the children. He sat down near Susan's shoes. Very softly and gently Susan reached down and scratched James under the chin and behind the ears.

"Purr," James said, and drooled a little on Susan's shoe.

"Oh, well!" said Thelma, having cleaned up the last of the cold roast beef. She arose in the air, flew over with great dignity, sat right down in Hank's lap, folded her wings, and said, "Purr, purr, purr . . ."

"Oh, Hank," Susan whispered, "their wings are furry."

"Oh, James," Harriet whispered, "their hands are kind."

FLAT STANLEY

written by Jeff Brown
illustrated by Tomi Ungerer

Breakfast was ready.

"I will go wake up the boys," Mrs. Lambchop said to her husband, George Lambchop. Just then their younger son, Arthur, called from the bedroom he shared with his brother Stanley.

"Hey! Come and look! Hey!"

Mr. and Mrs. Lambchop were both very much in favor of politeness and careful speech. "Hay is for horses, Arthur, not people," Mr. Lambchop said as they entered the bedroom. "Try to remember that."

"Excuse me," Arthur said. "But look!"

He pointed to Stanley's bed. Across it lay the enormous bulletin board that Mr. Lambchop had given the boys a Christmas ago, so that

they could pin up pictures and messages and maps. It had fallen, during the night, on top of Stanley.

But Stanley was not hurt. In fact he would still have been sleeping if he had not been woken by his brother's shout.

"What's going on here?" he called out cheerfully from beneath the enormous board.

Mr. and Mrs. Lambchop hurried to lift it from the bed.

"Heavens!" said Mrs. Lambchop.

"Gosh!" said Arthur. "Stanley's flat!"

"As a pancake," said Mr. Lambchop. "Darndest thing I've ever seen."

"Let's all have breakfast," Mrs. Lambchop said. "Then Stanley and I will go see Doctor Dan and hear what he has to say."

The examination was almost over.

"How do you feel?" Doctor Dan asked. "Does it hurt very much?"

"I felt sort of tickly for a while after I got up," Stanley Lambchop said, "but I feel fine now."

"Well, that's mostly how it is in these cases," said Doctor Dan.

"We'll just have to keep an eye on this young fellow," he said when he had finished the examination. "Sometimes we doctors, despite all our years of training and experience, can only marvel at how little we really know."

Mrs. Lambchop said she thought that Stanley's clothes would have to be altered by the tailor now, so Doctor Dan told his nurse to take Stanley's measurements.

Mrs. Lambchop wrote them down.

Stanley was four feet tall, about a foot wide, and half an inch thick.

When Stanley got used to being flat, he enjoyed it.

He could go in and out of rooms, even when the door was closed, just by lying down and sliding through the crack at the bottom.

Mr. and Mrs. Lambchop said it was silly, but they were quite proud of him.

Arthur got jealous and tried to slide under a door, but he just banged his head.

Being flat could also be helpful, Stanley found.

He was taking a walk with Mrs. Lambchop one afternoon when her favorite ring fell from her finger. The ring rolled across the sidewalk and down

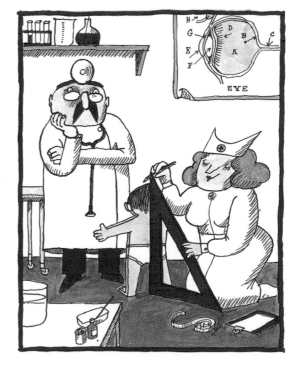

between the bars of a grating that covered a dark, deep shaft. Mrs. Lambchop began to cry.

"I have an idea," Stanley said.

He took the laces out of his shoes and an extra pair out of his pocket and tied them all together to make one long lace. Then he tied the end of that to the back of his belt and gave the other end to his mother.

"Lower me," he said, "and I will look for the ring."

"Thank you, Stanley," Mrs. Lambchop said. She lowered him between the bars and moved him carefully up and down and from side to side, so that he could search the whole floor of the shaft.

Two policemen came by and stared at Mrs. Lambchop as she stood holding the long lace that ran down through the grating. She pretended not to notice them.

"What's the matter, lady?" the first policeman asked. "Is your yo-yo stuck?"

"I am not playing with a yo-yo!" Mrs. Lambchop said sharply. "My son is at the other end of this lace, if you must know."

"Get the net, Harry," said the second policeman. "We have caught a cuckoo!"

Just then, down in the shaft, Stanley cried out, "Hooray!"

Mrs. Lambchop pulled him up and saw that he had the ring.

"Good for you, Stanley," she said. Then she turned angrily to the policemen.

"A cuckoo, indeed!" she said. "Shame!"

The policemen apologized. "We didn't get it, lady," they said. "We have been hasty. We see that now."

"People should think twice before making rude remarks," said Mrs. Lambchop. "And then not make them at all."

The policemen realized that was a good rule and said they would try to remember it.

One day Stanley got a letter from his friend Thomas Anthony Jeffrey, whose family had moved recently to California. A school vacation was about to begin and Stanley was invited to spend it with the Jeffreys.

"Oh, boy!" Stanley said. "I would love to go!"

Mr. Lambchop sighed. "A round-trip train or airplane ticket to California is very expensive," he said. "I will have to think of some cheaper way."

When Mr. Lambchop came home from the office that evening, he brought with him an enormous brown-paper envelope.

"Now then, Stanley," he said. "Try this for size."

The envelope fit Stanley very well. There was even room left over, Mrs. Lambchop discovered, for an egg-salad sandwich made with thin bread, and a flat cigarette case filled with milk.

They had to put a great many stamps on the envelope to pay for both airmail and insurance, but it was still much less expensive than a train

or airplane ticket to California would have been.

The next day Mr. and Mrs. Lambchop slid Stanley into his envelope, along with the egg-salad sandwich and the cigarette case full of milk, and mailed him from the box on the corner. The envelope had to be folded to fit through the slot, but Stanley was a limber boy and inside the box he straightened right up again.

Mrs. Lambchop was nervous because Stanley had never been away from home alone before. She rapped on the box.

"Can you hear me, dear?" she called. "Are you all right?"

Stanley's voice came quite clearly. "I'm fine. Can I eat my sandwich now?"

"Wait an hour. And try not to get overheated, dear," Mrs. Lambchop said. Then she and Mr. Lambchop cried out "Good-bye, good-bye!" and went home.

Stanley had a fine time in California. When the visit was over, the Jeffreys returned him in a beautiful white envelope they had made themselves. It had red-and-blue markings to show that it was airmail, and Thomas Jeffrey had lettered it VALUABLE and FRAGILE and THIS END UP on both sides.

Back home Stanley told his family that he had been handled so carefully he never felt a single bump. Mr. Lambchop said it proved that jet planes were wonderful, and so was the Post Office Department, and that this was a great age in which to live.

Stanley thought so too.

Mr. Lambchop had always liked to take the boys off with him on Sunday afternoons, to a museum or roller-skating in the park, but it was difficult when they were crossing streets or moving about in crowds. Stanley and Arthur would often be jostled from his side and Mr. Lambchop worried about speeding taxis or that hurrying people might accidentally knock them down.

It was easier after Stanley got flat.

Mr. Lambchop discovered that he could roll Stanley up without hurting him at all. He would tie a piece of string around Stanley to keep him from unrolling and make a little loop in the string for himself. It was as simple as carrying a parcel, and he could hold on to Arthur with the other hand.

Stanley did not mind being carried because he had never much liked to walk. Arthur didn't like to walk either, but he had to. It made him mad.

One Sunday afternoon, in the street, they met an old college friend of Mr. Lambchop's, a man he had not seen for years.

"Well, George, I see you have bought some wallpaper," the man said. "Going to decorate your house, I suppose?"

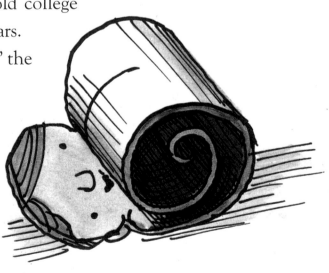

"Wallpaper?" said Mr. Lambchop. "Oh, no. This is my son Stanley."

He undid the string and Stanley unrolled.

"How do you do?" Stanley said.

"Nice to meet you, young feller," the man said. He said to Mr. Lambchop, "George, that boy is flat."

"Smart, too," Mr. Lambchop said. "Stanley is third from the top in his class at school."

"Phooey!" said Arthur.

"This is my younger son, Arthur," Mr. Lambchop said. "And he will apologize for his rudeness."

Arthur could only blush and apologize.

Mr. Lambchop rolled Stanley up again and they set out for home. It rained quite hard while they were on the way. Stanley, of course, hardly got wet at all, just around the edges, but Arthur got soaked.

Late that night Mr. and Mrs. Lambchop heard a noise out in the living room. They found Arthur lying on the floor near the bookcase. He had piled a great many volumes of the *Encyclopaedia Britannica* on top of himself.

"Put some more on me," Arthur said when he saw them. "Don't just stand there. Help me."

Mr. and Mrs. Lambchop sent him back to bed, but the next morning they spoke to Stanley. "Arthur can't help being jealous," they said. "Be nice to him. You're his big brother, after all."

Stanley and Arthur were in the park. The day was sunny, but windy too, and many older boys were flying beautiful, enormous kites with long tails, made in all the colors of the rainbow.

Arthur sighed. "Someday," he said, "I will have a big kite and I will win a kite-flying contest and be famous like everyone else. *Nobody* knows who I am these days."

Stanley remembered what his parents had said. He went to a boy whose kite was broken and borrowed a large spool of string.

"You can fly me, Arthur," he said. "Come on."

He attached the string to himself and gave Arthur the spool to hold. He ran lightly across the grass, sideways to get up speed, and then he turned to meet the breeze.

Up, up, up . . . UP! went Stanley, being a kite.

He knew just how to manage on the gusts of wind. He faced full into

the wind if he wanted to rise, and let it take him from
behind when he wanted speed. He had only to turn his thin
edge to the wind, carefully, a little at a time, so that it did
not hold him, and then he would slip gracefully down
toward the earth again.

Arthur let out all the string and Stanley soared high above
the trees, a beautiful sight, in his green sweater and brown
trousers, against the pale-blue sky.

Everyone in the park stood still to watch.

Stanley swooped right and then left in long, matched
swoops. He held his arms by his sides and zoomed at the
ground like a rocket and curved up again toward the sun.
He sideslipped and circled, and made figure eights and
crosses and a star.

Nobody has ever flown the way Stanley
Lambchop flew that day. Probably no one ever
will again.

After a while, of course, people grew
tired of watching and Arthur got tired of
running about with the empty spool.

Stanley went right on though, showing off.

Three boys came up to Arthur and invited him to join them for a hot dog and some soda pop. Arthur left the spool wedged in the fork of a tree. He did not notice, while he was eating the hot dog, that the wind was blowing the string and tangling it about the tree.

The string got shorter and shorter, but Stanley did not realize how low he was until leaves brushed his feet, and then it was too late. He got stuck in the branches. Fifteen minutes passed before Arthur and the other boys heard his cries and climbed up to set him free.

Stanley would not speak to his brother that evening, and at bedtime, even though Arthur had apologized, he was still cross.

Alone with Mr. Lambchop in the living room, Mrs. Lambchop sighed and shook her head. "You're at the office all day, having fun," she said. "You don't realize what I go through with the boys. They're very difficult."

"Kids are like that," Mr. Lambchop said. "Phases. Be patient, dear."

Mr. and Mrs. O. Jay Dart lived in the apartment above the Lambchops. Mr. Dart was an important man, the director of the Famous Museum of Art downtown in the city.

Stanley Lambchop had noticed in the elevator that Mr. Dart, who was ordinarily a cheerful man, had become quite gloomy, but he had no idea what the reason was. And then at breakfast one morning he heard Mr. and Mrs. Lambchop talking about Mr. Dart.

"I see," said Mr. Lambchop, reading the paper over his coffee cup, "that still another painting has been stolen from the Famous Museum. A Toulouse-Lautrec."

Mrs. Lambchop sipped her coffee. "That probably made it easy to steal," she said. "Being too loose, I mean."

"It says," Mr. Lambchop went on, "that Mr. O. Jay Dart, the director, is at his wits' end. The police are no help. Listen to what the Chief of Police told the newspaper. 'We suspect a gang of sneak thieves. These are the worst kind. They work by sneakery, which makes them very difficult to catch. However, my men and I will keep trying. Meanwhile, I hope people will buy tickets for the Policemen's Ball and not park their cars where signs say don't.'"

The next morning Stanley Lambchop heard Mr. Dart talking to his wife in the elevator.

"These sneak thieves work at night," Mr. Dart said. "It is very hard for our guards to stay awake when they have been on duty all day. And the Famous Museum is so big we cannot guard every picture at the same time. I fear it is hopeless, hopeless, hopeless!"

Suddenly, as if an electric light bulb had lit up in the air above his head, giving out little shooting lines of excitement, Stanley Lambchop had an idea. He told it to Mr. Dart.

"Stanley," Mr. Dart said, "if your mother will give her permission, I will put you and your plan to work this very night!"

Mrs. Lambchop gave her permission. "But you will have to take a long nap this afternoon," she said. "I won't have you up till all hours unless you do."

That evening, after a long nap, Stanley went with Mr. Dart to the Famous Museum. Mr. Dart took him into the main hall, where the biggest and most important paintings were hung. He pointed to a huge painting that showed a bearded man, wearing a floppy velvet hat, playing a violin for a lady who lay on a couch. There was a half-man, half-horse person standing behind them, and three fat children with wings were flying around above. That, Mr. Dart explained, was the most expensive painting in the world!

There was an empty picture frame on the opposite wall. We shall hear more about that later on.

Mr. Dart took Stanley into his office and said, "It is time for you to put on a disguise."

"I already thought of that," Stanley Lambchop said, "and I brought one. My cowboy suit. It has a red bandanna that I can tie over my face. Nobody will recognize me in a million years."

"No," Mr. Dart said. "You will have to wear the disguise I have chosen."

From a closet he took out a white dress with a blue sash, a pair of shiny little pointed shoes, a wide straw hat with a blue band that matched the sash, and a wig and a stick. The wig was made of blond hair, long and done in ringlets. The stick was curved at the top and it, too, had a blue ribbon on it.

"In this shepherdess disguise," Mr. Dart said, "you will look like a painting that belongs in the main hall. We do not have cowboy pictures in the main hall."

Stanley was so disgusted he could hardly speak. "I will look like a girl, that's what I will look like," he said. "I wish I had never had my idea."

But he was a good sport, so he put on the disguise.

Back in the main hall Mr. Dart helped Stanley climb up into the empty picture frame. Stanley was able to stay in place because Mr. Dart had cleverly put four small spikes in the wall, one for each hand and foot.

The frame was a perfect fit. Against the wall, Stanley looked just like a picture.

"Except for one thing," Mr. Dart said. "Shepherdesses are supposed to look happy. They smile at their sheep and at the sky. You look fierce, not happy, Stanley."

Stanley tried to get a faraway look in his eyes and even to smile a bit.

Mr. Dart stood back a few feet and stared at him for a moment.

"Well," he said, "it may not be art, but I know what I like."

He went off to make sure that certain other parts of Stanley's plan were being taken care of, and Stanley was left alone.

It was very dark in the main hall. A little bit of moonlight came through the windows, and Stanley could just make out the world's most expensive painting on the opposite wall. He felt as though the bearded man with the violin and the lady on the couch and the half-horse person and the winged children were all waiting, as he was, for something to happen.

Time passed and he got tireder and tireder. Anyone would be tired this late at night, especially if he had to stand in a picture frame balancing on little spikes.

Maybe they won't come, Stanley thought. Maybe the sneak thieves won't come at all.

The moon went behind a cloud and then the main hall was pitch dark. It seemed to get quieter, too, with the darkness. There was absolutely no sound at all. Stanley felt the hair on the back of his neck prickle beneath the golden curls of the wig.

Cr-eee-eee-k . . .

The creaking sound came from right out in the middle of the main hall and even as he heard it Stanley saw, in the same place, a tiny yellow glow of light!

The creaking came again and the glow grew bigger. A trap door had opened in the floor and two men came up through it into the hall!

Stanley understood everything all at once. These must be the sneak thieves! They had a secret trap door entrance into the museum from outside. That was why they had never been caught. And now, tonight, they were back to steal the most expensive painting in the world!

He held very still in his picture frame and listened to the sneak thieves.

"This is it, Max," said the first one. "This is where we art robbers pull a sensational job whilst the civilized community sleeps."

"Right, Luther," said the other man. "In all this great city there is no one to suspicion us."

Ha, ha! thought Stanley Lambchop. That's what you think!

The sneak thieves put down their lantern and took the world's most expensive painting off the wall.

"What would we do to anyone who tried to capture us, Max?" the first man asked.

"We would kill him. What else?" his friend replied.

That was enough to frighten Stanley, and he was even more frightened when Luther came over and stared at him.

"This sheep girl," Luther said. "I thought sheep girls were supposed to smile, Max. This one looks scared."

Just in time, Stanley managed to get a faraway look in his eyes again and to smile, sort of.

"You're crazy, Luther," Max said. "She's smiling. And what a pretty little thing she is, too."

That made Stanley furious. He waited until the sneak thieves had turned back to the world's most expensive painting, and then he shouted in his loudest, most terrifying voice: "POLICE! POLICE! MR. DART! THE SNEAK THIEVES ARE HERE!"

The sneak thieves looked at each other. "Max," said the first one, very quietly, "I think I heard the sheep girl yell."

"I think I did too," said Max in a quivery voice. "Oh, boy! Yelling pictures. We both need a rest."

"You'll get a rest, all right!" shouted Mr. Dart, rushing in with the Chief of Police and lots of guards and policemen behind him. "You'll get *ar-rested*, that's what! Ha, ha, ha!"

The sneak thieves were too mixed up by Mr. Dart's joke and too frightened by the policemen to put up a fight. Before they knew it, they had been handcuffed and led away to jail.

The next morning in the office of the Chief of Police, Stanley Lambchop got a medal. The day after that his picture was in all the newspapers.

For a while Stanley Lambchop was a famous name. Everywhere that Stanley went, people stared and pointed at him. He could hear them whisper, "Over there, Harriet, over there! That must be Stanley Lambchop, the one who caught the sneak thieves..." and things like that.

But after a few weeks the whispering and the staring stopped. People had other things to think about. Stanley did not mind. Being famous had been fun, but enough was enough.

And then came a further change, and it was not a pleasant one. People began to laugh and make fun of him as he passed by. "Hello, Super-Skinny!" they would shout, and even ruder things, about the way he looked.

Stanley told his parents how he felt. "It's the other kids I mostly mind," he said. "They don't like me anymore because I'm different. Flat."

"Shame on them," Mrs. Lambchop said. "It is wrong to dislike people for their shapes. Or their religion, for that matter, or the color of their skin."

"I know," Stanley said. "Only maybe it's impossible for everybody to like *everybody*."

"Perhaps," said Mrs. Lambchop. "But they can try."

Later that night Arthur Lambchop was woken by the sound of crying. In the darkness he crept across the room and knelt by Stanley's bed.

"Are you okay?" he said.

"Go away," Stanley said.

"Don't be mad at me," Arthur said. "You're still mad because I let you get tangled the day you were my kite, I guess."

"Skip it, will you?" Stanley said. "I'm not mad. Go away."

"Please let's be friends..." Arthur couldn't help crying a little, too. "Oh, Stanley," he said. "Please tell me what's wrong?"

Stanley waited for a long time before he spoke. "The thing is," he said, "I'm just not happy anymore. I'm tired of being flat. I want to be a regular shape again, like other people. But I'll have to go on being flat forever. It makes me sick."

"Oh, Stanley," Arthur said. He dried his tears on a corner of Stanley's sheet and could think of nothing more to say.

"Don't talk about what I just said," Stanley told him. "I don't want the folks to worry. That would only make it worse."

"You're brave," Arthur said. "You really are."

He took hold of Stanley's hand. The two brothers sat together in the darkness, being friends. They were both still sad, but each one felt a *little* better than he had before.

And then, suddenly, though he was not even trying to think, Arthur had an idea. He jumped up and turned on the light and ran to the big storage box where toys and things were kept. He began to rummage in the box.

Stanley sat up in bed to watch.

Arthur flung aside a football and some lead soldiers and airplane models and lots of wooden blocks, and then he said, "Aha!" He had found what he wanted—an old bicycle pump. He held it up, and Stanley and he looked at each other.

"Okay," Stanley said at last. "But take it easy." He put the end of the long pump hose in his mouth and clamped his lips tightly about it so that no air could escape.

"I'll go slowly," Arthur said. "If it hurts or anything, wiggle your hand at me."

He began to pump. At first nothing happened except that Stanley's cheeks bulged a bit. Arthur watched his hand, but there was no wiggle signal, so he pumped on. Then, suddenly, Stanley's top half began to swell.

"It's working! It's working!" shouted Arthur, pumping away.

Stanley spread his arms so that the air could get around inside of him more easily. He got bigger and bigger. The buttons of his pajama top burst off—*Pop! Pop! Pop!* A moment more and he was all rounded out; head and body, arms and legs. But not his right foot. That foot stayed flat.

Arthur stopped pumping. "It's like trying to do the very last bit of those long balloons," he said. "Maybe a shake would help."

Stanley shook his right foot twice, and with a little *whooshing* sound it swelled out to match the left one. There stood Stanley Lambchop as he used to be, as if he had never been flat at all!

"Thank you, Arthur," Stanley said. "Thank you very much."

The brothers were shaking hands when Mr. Lambchop strode into the room with Mrs. Lambchop right behind him. "We heard you!" said Mr. Lambchop. "Up and talking when you ought to be asleep, eh? Shame on—"

"GEORGE!" said Mrs. Lambchop. "Stanley's *round* again!"

"You're right!" said Mr. Lambchop, noticing. "Good for you, Stanley!"

"I'm the one who did it," Arthur said. "I blew him up."

Everyone was terribly excited and happy, of course. Mrs. Lambchop made hot chocolate to celebrate the occasion, and several toasts were drunk to Arthur for his cleverness.

When the little party was over, Mr. and Mrs. Lambchop tucked the boys back into their beds and kissed them, and then they turned out the light.

"Good night," they said.

"Good night," said Stanley and Arthur.

It had been a long and tiring day. Very soon all the Lambchops were asleep.

LITTLE TIM AND THE BRAVE SEA CAPTAIN

written and illustrated by Edward Ardizzone

Little Tim lived in a house by the sea. He wanted very much to be a sailor.

When it was fine he spent the day on the beach playing in and out of the boats, or talking to his friend the old boatman, who taught him how to make the special knots that sailors make and many other things about the sea and ships.

Sometimes Tim would astonish his parents by saying, "That's a Cunarder" or "Look at that barquentine on the port bow."

When it was wet or too cold and rough to play on the beach, Tim would visit his old friend, Captain McFee.

The Captain would tell him about his voyages and sometimes give him a sip of his grog, which made Tim want to be a sailor more than ever.

But alas for Tim's hopes. When he asked his mother and father if he could be a sailor, they laughed and said he was much too young, and must wait for years and years until he was grown up. This made Tim very sad.

In fact he was so sad that he resolved, at the first opportunity, to run away to sea.

Now one day, the old boatman told Tim that he was going out in his motor boat to a steamer which was anchored in the bay.

Would Tim like to come, too, and lend him a hand with the boat?

Tim was overjoyed.

The boatman went on to say that the captain of the steamer was an old friend of his, and, as the steamer was about to sail, he wanted to say "good-bye" to him.

Tim made himself very useful, helping to stow gear into the boat, fill the petrol tank, and make all ready to go to sea.

When this was done, the boatman said, "Come, give a shove, my lad," and they both pushed the boat down the shingle beach into the water, then clambered on board, and off they went.

It was a lovely day. The sea was blue, and the little waves danced and sparkled in the sunshine.

Tim got more and more excited as they neared the steamer, as he had never been in one before.

When they arrived alongside they clambered on board.

Tim was left on deck while the boatman went to see the captain, who was in his cabin.

Now Tim had a great idea. He would hide, and, when the boatman left, not seeing Tim, he would forget all about him.

This is exactly what happened.

Off went the boatman and away went the steamer with Tim on board.

When Tim thought there was no chance of being put on shore he showed himself to a sailor.

"Oi!" said the sailor. "What are you doing on here? Come along with me, my lad, the captain will have something to say to you."

When the captain saw Tim he was furious and said Tim was a stowaway and must be made to work his passage.

So they gave Tim a pail and a scrubbing brush and made him scrub the deck, which Tim found very hard work. It made his back ache and his fingers sore. He cried quite a lot and wished he had never run away to sea.

After what seemed hours to Tim, the sailor came and said he could stop work and that he had not done too badly for a lad of his size. He then took Tim to the galley where the cook gave him a mug of cocoa.

Tim felt better after the cocoa, and when the sailor found him a bunk, he climbed in and was soon fast asleep. He was so tired he did not even bother to take off his clothes.

Tim soon got accustomed to life on board. As he was a bright boy and always ready to make himself useful, it was not long before he became popular with the crew. Even the captain said he was not too bad for a stowaway.

Tim's best friend was the cook, who was a family man. Tim would help him peel potatoes, wash up and tidy the galley, and in return the cook would give Tim any nice titbits that were going.

Besides helping the cook, Tim would run errands and do all sorts of odd jobs, such as taking the captain his dinner and the second mate his grog, helping the man at the wheel and sewing buttons on the sailors' trousers.

One morning the wind began to blow hard and the sea became rough, which made the steamer rock like anything.

At first Tim rather enjoyed this. It excited him to watch the big waves and see the crew hurrying about the deck making everything shipshape and secure.

But alas, Tim soon began to feel sick, and when he went down to the galley he could not eat any of the titbits that the cook gave him.

All that day it blew harder and harder and the sea became rougher and rougher till by nightfall it was blowing a terrible gale.

Poor Tim felt so sick that all he could do was to creep into his bunk and lie there, wishing he had never gone to sea.

In the middle of the night there was a terrible crash. The ship had

Little Tim and the Brave Sea Captain   145

struck a rock and lay on its side with the great waves pouring over it.

The sailors rushed on deck shouting, "We are sinking. To the boats. To the boats!"

With great difficulty they launched the boats and away they went in the raging sea.

—BUT—

—they had quite forgotten Tim. He was so small and frightened that nobody had noticed him.

Tim crept onto the bridge where he found the captain, who had refused to leave his ship.

"Hullo, my lad," said the captain. "Come, stop crying and be a brave boy. We are bound for Davy Jones's locker and tears won't help us now."

So Tim dried his eyes and tried not to be too frightened. He felt he would not mind going anywhere with the captain, even to Davy Jones's locker.

They stood hand in hand and waited for the end.

Just as they were about to sink beneath the waves Tim gave a great cry. "We're saved. We're saved."

He had seen a lifeboat coming to rescue them.

The lifeboat came alongside and a lifeline was thrown to them.

Down the lifeline, first Tim and then the captain were drawn to safety. But only just in time.

Hardly had they left the steamer when it sank beneath the waves.

Now followed a terrible journey through the raging sea.

The lifeboat was tossed about like a cork by the great waves which often dashed over the side and soaked them to the skin.

It was many hours before they neared land, and all were very cold and wet and tired.

When the lifeboat came into harbor, the crowd, which had gathered on the quay to watch its return, gave a great cheer. They had seen Tim and the captain and had realized that the lifeboat had made a gallant rescue.

As soon as the lifeboat had moored beside the quay, Tim was lifted out and he and the captain were taken to the nearest house.

Here they were wrapped in blankets and sat in front of the fire with their feet in tubs of hot water. Also they were given cups of hot cocoa and so were soon nice and warm, both inside and out.

Once they were warm right through they were put to bed.

They were still very tired from their terrible adventure, so they slept for hours and hours.

When they woke up the next morning, however, they both felt rested and were glad to be alive and well.

Tim hurried to send a telegram to his parents saying he was taking the train home and that the captain was coming, too.

Then he and the captain, after thanking the lifeboatmen and the kind people who had put them up, went to the station and caught their train.

On the platform they were surprised to see a large crowd waiting to see them off.

Among the crowd were many ladies who kissed Tim and gave him chocolate and fruit to eat on the journey.

Tim felt very excited and could not help feeling a bit of a hero.

But Tim became even more excited as the train neared his home town.

He had his nose glued to the window all the time looking out for familiar places and pointing them out to the captain when he saw them.

Tim's parents were at the garden gate when they arrived.

Captain McFee and the boatman were there, too.

You can imagine how pleased Tim was to see his father and mother and his old friends again.

The captain told Tim's parents all about their adventures and how brave Tim had been, and he asked them if they would let Tim come with him on his next voyage as he felt that Tim had the makings of a fine sailor.

Tim was very pleased and happy to hear his parents say yes.

The lifeboatmen were pleased, too, as they were presented by the Mayor with medals for bravery.

FRECKLE JUICE

written by Judy Blume
illustrated by Sonia O. Lisker

CHAPTER ONE

Andrew Marcus wanted freckles. Nicky Lane had freckles. He had about a million of them. They covered his face, his ears and the back of his neck. Andrew didn't have any freckles. He had two warts on his finger. But they didn't do him any good at all. If he had freckles like Nicky, his mother would never know if his neck was dirty. So he wouldn't have to wash. And then he'd never be late for school.

Andrew had plenty of time to look at Nicky's freckles. He sat right behind him in class. Once he even tried to count them. But when he got to eighty-six Miss Kelly called, "Andrew . . . are you paying attention?"

"Yes, Miss Kelly," Andrew said.

"Good, Andrew. I'm glad to hear that. Now will you please pick up your chair and join your reading group? We're all waiting for you."

Andrew stood up in a hurry. His reading group giggled. Especially Sharon. He couldn't stand that Sharon. She thought she knew everything! He picked up his chair and carried it to the corner where his reading group sat.

"You may begin, Andrew," Miss Kelly said. "Page sixty-four."

Andrew turned the pages in his book. Sixty-four . . . sixty-four. He couldn't find it. The pages stuck together. Why did Miss Kelly have to pick him? Everybody else already had their books opened to the right page.

Sharon kept giggling. She covered her mouth to keep in the noise, but Andrew knew what was going on. He finally found page sixty-four. Right where it was supposed to be . . . between pages sixty-three and sixty-five. If he had his own freckles he wouldn't have to count Nicky Lane's. Then he'd hear Miss Kelly when she called reading groups. And nobody would laugh at him.

Later, when the bell rang, Andrew poked Nicky Lane.

"What do you want?" Nicky asked, turning around.

"I was wondering about your freckles," Andrew said.

"Oh yeah? What about them?"

Andrew felt pretty stupid. "Well, how did you get them?"

"What do you mean *how*? You get *born* with them. That's how!"

Andrew thought that's what Nicky would say. Some help *he* was!

"Line up, boys and girls," Miss Kelly said. "Time to go home now. Sharon, you may lead the girls. Andrew, you may lead the boys."

Some luck! Just when he got to be leader he had to stand next to *Sharon*!

When they were in line Sharon whispered to Andrew. "Psst . . . I know how to get them."

"How to get what?" Andrew asked.

"Freckles," Sharon said.

"Who asked *you*?"

"I heard you ask Nicky about his." Sharon ran her tongue along her teeth. She was always doing that.

"Do you want to know how to get them?" Sharon asked.

"Maybe," Andrew told her.

"It'll cost you fifty cents. I have a secret recipe for freckle juice," Sharon whispered.

"A secret recipe?"

"Uh huh."

Sharon's tongue reminded Andrew of a frog catching flies.

He wondered if Sharon ever got a mouthful of bugs the way she opened her mouth and wiggled her tongue around. Andrew inspected Sharon's face. "You don't even have freckles!" he said.

"Look close," Sharon said. "I've got six on my nose."

"Big deal! A lot of good six'll do."

"You can get as many as you want. Six was enough for me. It all depends on how much freckle juice you drink."

Andrew didn't believe Sharon for a minute. Not one minute! There was no such thing as freckle juice. Andrew had never heard of it before!

CHAPTER TWO

That night Andrew had trouble sleeping. He kept thinking about freckle juice. Maybe the reason no one in his family had freckles was because no one knew the secret recipe. If they never even heard of freckle juice, then how could they have any freckles? It figured!

Andrew didn't like the idea of paying Sharon for anything. And fifty cents was a lot of money. It was five whole weeks of allowance! But he decided that if Sharon's recipe didn't work he'd ask for his money back. It was easy.

The next morning Andrew turned the combination of his safe-bank to just the right numbers. Four on top and zero on the bottom. He took out five dimes. He wrapped them in a tissue and stuffed the whole thing in his pocket. He didn't have time to wash his ears or neck or anything. He wanted to see Sharon before the last bell rang.

"Bye Mom," Andrew called.

"Andrew Marcus! Wait a minute!" His mother hurried over to him. She almost tripped on her long bathrobe. The curlers in her hair scratched Andrew's face as she checked his ears and neck.

"Please Mom! Can't we skip it just this once?" Andrew begged.

Mrs. Marcus stepped away from Andrew. She pointed a finger at him. "Okay," she said. "I'll let you go this time. But tomorrow I'm looking again. And, Andrew, zip up your pants."

Andrew looked down. Zippers were a pain!

"This afternoon when you come home I'll be next door. Mrs. Burrows invited me over to play cards. You come get the key from me, okay?"

"Sure Mom. Okay."

Andrew raced to school. He could hardly wait to see the secret recipe. First he'd look at it, and if it didn't seem any good, he just wouldn't pay.

Sharon was already at her desk when Andrew arrived. He went right over to her.

"Did you bring it?" he asked.

"Bring what?" Sharon opened her eyes real wide.

"You know what! The secret recipe for freckle juice."

"Oh that! I have it—right here." Sharon patted her pocket.

"Well, let's see it."

"Do you have the fifty cents?" Sharon asked.

"Sure—right here." Andrew patted *his* pocket.

"I'm not going to show it to you until you pay," Sharon said.

Andrew shook his head. "Oh no! First I want to see it."

"Sorry, Andrew. A deal's a deal!" Sharon opened a book and pretended to read.

"Andrew Marcus!" Miss Kelly said. "Will you please sit down. The second bell just rang. This morning we'll begin with arithmetic. Nicky, please pass out the yellow paper. When you get your paper begin working on the problems on the board."

Andrew went to his seat. Then he took the tissue with five dimes out of his pocket. He held it near the floor and aimed it toward Sharon.

She sat in the next row. Sharon stuck out her foot and stepped on the tissue. Then she slid it over until she could reach it with her hand.

She bent down and picked it up. Miss Kelly didn't notice.

Sharon counted the five dimes. Then she took a  piece of folded-up white paper out of her pocket and threw it to Andrew.

 It landed in the middle of the aisle. Andrew leaned way over to pick it up. But he lost his balance and fell off his chair.

Everybody laughed, except Andrew and Miss Kelly.

Miss Kelly sighed. "Oh Andrew! What are you up to *now*? Bring that note, please."

Andrew picked up the secret recipe. He didn't even have a chance to see it. It wasn't fair. It cost him fifty cents for nothing. He handed it to Miss Kelly. She read it. Then she looked up at him. "Andrew, you may have this back at three o'clock." She put it in her desk. "I don't want this to happen again. Do you understand?"

"Yes, Miss Kelly," Andrew mumbled.

"Good. Now let's get the arithmetic done."

Miss Kelly wasn't bad, Andrew decided. She could have ripped up the recipe. Or sent him to the principal's office. Or even made him stand outside in the hall by himself.

Andrew could hardly wait for three o'clock to come. He didn't bother counting Nicky Lane's freckles. Soon he'd have his own. When the second bell finally rang and the class marched down the hall, Andrew went up to Miss Kelly. She held the piece of white paper and waved it at him.

"Here's your note, Andrew. I have the feeling it's important to you. But from now on you must pay attention in class."

Andrew took the recipe from Miss Kelly. "After tomorrow I won't have any trouble paying attention," he promised. "Just you wait, Miss Kelly. I won't have any trouble at all!"

CHAPTER THREE

Andrew ran all the way home. Then he remembered he had to go to Mrs. Burrows' house to get the key. The secret recipe for freckle juice was folded carefully in the bottom of Andrew's shoe. He was going to put it inside his sock, but he was afraid if his foot got sweaty the ink might blur and he wouldn't be able to read it. So, inside his shoe was safe enough. Even if it was windy nothing could happen to it there. He made up his mind not to read it until he got home. He didn't want to waste any time getting there. And he wasn't the world's fastest reader anyway, even though he'd gotten better since last fall. Still, there might be some hard words that would take a while to figure out.

Andrew pressed Mrs. Burrows' doorbell.

"Hello, Andrew," she said when she opened the door. "You're home from school early."

"I ran all the way," Andrew panted.

"How about some milk and cookies?" Mrs. Burrows asked.

"No thank you. I just want the key."

"Well, come in, Andrew. Your mother's in the living room."

Andrew followed Mrs. Burrows. His mother was dealing four piles of cards.

"Hi Mom. I came for the key."

"Manners, Andrew . . . manners! Don't you say hello to all the ladies?" Mrs. Marcus asked.

"Oh. Hello," Andrew said.

Mrs. Marcus reached for her purse. She opened it and gave Andrew the key. "Change your clothes and play outside. I'll be home by four o'clock."

That only gave him an hour. He hoped the recipe didn't say to cook anything. He wasn't allowed to turn on the stove or the oven. Andrew dashed to his house, unlocked the front door and took off his shoe as soon as he was inside. He pulled out the secret recipe and sat down on the floor to read it. It said:

SHARON'S Secret Recipe for Freckle Juice

One glass makes an average amount of freckles. To get like Nicky Lane drink two glasses. Mix up all these things together— stir well and drink fast. grape juice, vinegar, mustard, mayonnaise, juice from one lemon, pepper and salt, ketchup, olive oil, and a speck of onion.

P.S. The faster you drink it the faster you get

F·R·E·C·K·L·E·S

Andrew read the list twice. It didn't sound like much of a secret recipe. His mother used those things every day. Of course, she didn't use them all *together*. Maybe that was the secret part. Well, he'd paid fifty cents. He might as well find out.

He climbed up on the kitchen counter so he could reach the cabinets.

He found everything except the lemon—that was in the refrigerator—and the onion. Mrs. Marcus kept onions in the basement in a bin. Andrew ran downstairs and selected a small one, since the recipe only called for a speck. With or without the skin, Andrew wondered.

He chose a big blue glass. He'd start with just one glassful and then drink another if he wanted more freckles. No point in overdoing it the first time. That's what his mother always said.

Now, first the grape juice, Andrew thought. He filled the glass halfway and added an ice cube. All drinks tasted better cold and he was sure this one would too.

Then he added the other ingredients one by one. His mother had two kinds of vinegars—wine vinegar and plain vinegar. Andrew picked the wine one. He put in some hot mustard, one spoonful of mayonnaise and plenty of pepper and salt. Then some ketchup . . . that was hard to pour. But what about olive oil? His mother had vegetable oil, but no olive oil. Maybe the stuff that looked like water in the olive jar was what Sharon meant. He put in a few spoonfuls of that. Now for the lemon. Andrew cut one in half and squeezed. Oh no! A seed dropped in by mistake. He picked it out with his spoon. He hated pits in his juice. Now all he needed was that speck of onion and he was all set. He stirred up the drink and smelled it.

OH! IT SMELLED AWFUL! JUST PLAIN AWFUL! He'd have to hold his nose while he drank it. He stuck his tongue into the glass to taste it. Ick! *Terrible!* He didn't know how he would ever manage to get it down . . . and fast too. It said to drink it very fast! That old Sharon! She probably thought he wouldn't be able to drink it. Well, he'd show her. He'd drink it all right!

Andrew held his nose, tilted his head back and gulped down Sharon's secret recipe for freckle juice. He felt like throwing up . . . it was that bad! But if he did he'd never get freckles. No, he would be strong!

Andrew crept into his mother's bedroom. He didn't feel well enough to walk. He sat on the floor in front of the full-length mirror. He waited for something to happen.

CHAPTER FOUR

Pretty soon something happened, all right. Andrew turned greenish and felt very sick. His stomach hurt. At four o'clock Mrs. Marcus came home.

"Yoo hoo . . . Andrew. Where are you?" she called.

Andrew heard her but he couldn't answer. He was too weak. He made a small noise.

"Andrew Marcus! Is that you?" His mother stood in the doorway of her bedroom. "What are you doing in here? I told you to play outside! And why didn't you change your clothes? Didn't I say to change your clothes?"

Andrew made another noise. Mrs. Marcus looked at his face. "Andrew you're green. *Absolutely green!* Are you sick?"

Andrew nodded. He was afraid if he opened his mouth he'd lose the freckle juice.

"What hurts?" Mrs. Marcus asked, feeling his forehead.

Andrew moaned and held his stomach.

"Oh my! Appendicitis! *You must have appendicitis.* I'm going to call the doctor. No, I'd better just drive straight to the hospital. No, I'll call the ambulance!"

Andrew shook his head but his mother didn't notice.

She said, "Don't move. I'm going into the kitchen to phone. I'll be right back."

Andrew rolled around, moaning.

Mrs. Marcus came back to her bedroom in a hurry. "Andrew Marcus! I've just seen the mess in the kitchen. Did you or did you not make something and eat it?"

Oh-oh! He forgot to clean up. Now she knew. Well, he didn't care. His stomach was killing him.

"Well, young man! I'm surprised at you. *Surprised!* Mrs. Burrows offered you milk and cookies and you refused. Then you came home and made yourself an . . . an I-don't-know-what and scared me half to death thinking you had appendicitis. I always thought you were more sensible, Andrew! I just can't believe it."

Andrew closed his eyes.

"Now, young man . . . *you* are going to *bed!*"

Andrew thought that was the best idea he'd heard in a long time. Mrs. Marcus gave him two spoonfuls of pink stuff that tasted like peppermint. Then she tucked him into bed.

Maybe the freckles would come out while he was sleeping. Right now he didn't care much if they *ever* came out! He hated Sharon. She'd done it on purpose. Just to get his fifty cents! He'd show her. She'd be sorry some day. He drifted off to sleep. He had terrible dreams. A big green monster made him drink two quarts of freckle juice, three times a day. Every time he drank it, the *monster* got freckles but Andrew didn't.

Andrew woke up sweaty. His stomach still felt funny. His mother gave him two more spoonfuls of that pink stuff and he fell asleep again.

The next day Andrew stayed home from school. He only looked in the mirror once—no freckles! He wasn't surprised. At noon he drank some hot tea. He wasn't ever going back to school. Sharon wasn't going to see him without freckles. She thought she was so great. Well, she wasn't going to get the chance to laugh at him. No sir!

But the following day his mother woke him up and sang, "Time for school. Rise and shine! Don't forget to wash your neck and behind your ears." She pulled the covers off him.

"I'm not going to school today," Andrew said. "I'm never going to school again." He hid his head under his pillow.

"So! I've got a school dropout in second grade. We'll have to do something about that! Here are your clothes. I want to see you up and dressed before I count to fifteen or you're going to take three baths a day *every* day for the next ten years!"

Andrew got dressed. He ate a breakfast bun and drank some milk. But he couldn't let Sharon get away with it. He had to do something!

CHAPTER FIVE

After breakfast Andrew raced back to his bedroom. He opened his desk drawer and looked for a brown magic marker. All he could find was a blue one. It was getting late. Blue would have to do. He put the magic marker in his lunch box and headed for school. He stopped two blocks before he got there. He studied his reflection in a car window. Then he took out the magic marker and decorated his whole face and neck with blue dots. Maybe they didn't look like Nicky Lane's freckles, but they sure looked like something!

Andrew waited until the second bell rang. Then he hurried to his class and sat down. He took out a book and tried to read it. He heard a lot of whispering but he didn't look up.

Miss Kelly snapped her fingers. "Let's settle down, children. Stop chattering." Everybody giggled. "What's so funny? Just what is so *funny*? Lisa, can you tell me the joke?"

Lisa stood up. "It's Andrew, Miss Kelly. Just look at Andrew Marcus!"

"Stand up, Andrew. Let me have a look at you," Miss Kelly said.

Andrew stood up.

"Good heavens, Andrew! What have you *done* to yourself?"

"I grew freckles, Miss Kelly. That's what!" Andrew knew his blue dots looked silly but he didn't care. He turned toward Sharon and stuck out his tongue. Sharon made a frog face at him.

Miss Kelly took a deep breath. "I see," she said. "You may sit down now, Andrew. Let's get on with our morning work."

At recess Nicky Lane turned around and said, "Whoever heard of blue freckles?"

Andrew didn't answer him. He sat in class all day with his blue freckles. A couple of times Miss Kelly looked at him kind of funny but she didn't say anything. Then at two o'clock she called him to her desk.

"Andrew," Miss Kelly said. "How would you like to use my secret formula for removing freckles?" Her voice was low, but not so low that the class couldn't hear.

"For free?" Andrew asked.

"Oh yes," Miss Kelly said. "For free."

Andrew scratched his head and thought it over.

Miss Kelly took a small package out of her desk. She handed it to Andrew. "Now, don't open this until you get to the Boys' Room. Remember, it's a *secret formula*. Okay?"

"Okay," Andrew said.

He wanted to run to the Boys' Room, but he knew the rules. No running in the halls. So he walked as fast as he could. He couldn't wait to see what was in the package. Could there really be such a thing as freckle remover?

As soon as he was inside the Boys' Room he unwrapped the package. There was a note. Andrew read it. It said:

TURN ON WATER. WET MAGIC FRECKLE REMOVER AND RUB INTO FACE. RINSE. IF MAGIC FRECKLE REMOVER DOES NOT WORK FIRST TIME . . . TRY AGAIN. THREE TIMES SHOULD DO THE JOB.

MISS KELLY

Ha! Miss Kelly knew. She knew all the time. She knew his freckles weren't really freckles. But she didn't tell. Andrew followed Miss Kelly's directions. The magic freckle remover formula smelled like lemons. Andrew had to use it four times to get his freckles off. Then he wrapped it up and walked back to his classroom.

Miss Kelly smiled. "Well, Andrew. I see it worked."

"Yes, Miss Kelly. It sure did."

"You look fine now, Andrew. You know, I think you're a very handsome boy without freckles!"

"You *do?*"

"Yes, I do."

"Miss Kelly . . . Miss Kelly!" Nicky Lane called out, raising his hand and waving it all around.

"What is it, Nicky?" Miss Kelly asked.

"Could I use your magic freckle remover? Could I, Miss Kelly? I hate my freckles. I hate every single one of them."

Andrew couldn't believe it. How could Nicky hate his freckles? They were so neat!

"Nicky," Miss Kelly said. "Andrew didn't look good with freckles. But you look wonderful! I'd hate to see you without them. They're part of you. So, I'm going to put away this magic formula. I hope I never have to use it again."

Well, Andrew thought. She'd never have to use it on *him*. He was *through* with freckles.

When the class lined up to go home Andrew heard Sharon whisper to Nicky. "I know how to get rid of them."

"Get rid of what?" Nicky asked.

"Your freckles."

"You do?"

"Sure. The secret recipe for removing freckles has been in my family for years. That's how come none of us have any. I'll sell it to you for fifty cents!"

Then Sharon walked up alongside Andrew. Before Andrew could say a word Sharon made a super-duper frog face just for him.

TELL ME A MITZI

written by Lore Segal
illustrated by Harriet Pincus

MITZI TAKES A TAXI

"*T*ell me a story," said Martha.

Once upon a time (*said her mother*) there was a Mitzi. She had a mother and a father and a brother who was a baby. His name was Jacob.

One morning Mitzi woke up. Jacob was in his crib, asleep. Mitzi went and looked in her mother and father's room. They were asleep.

She looked in the living room. There was nobody there. There was nobody in the kitchen.

Mitzi went back into the children's room, shook the crib and said, "Jacob, are you asleep?"

Jacob said, "Dadadadada."

"Good," said Mitzi. "What shall we do?"

"Let's go to Grandma and Grandpa's house," said Jacob.

"Right," said Mitzi. "Let's go."

"First make me my bottle," said Jacob. So Mitzi got Jacob's bottle, carried it into the kitchen and opened the refrigerator and took out a carton of milk and opened it and took the top off Jacob's

bottle and poured in the milk and put the top back on and closed the carton and put it back in the refrigerator and closed the door and carried the bottle into the children's room and gave it to Jacob and said, "Let's go."

Jacob said, "Change my diaper." So Mitzi climbed into Jacob's crib and took his pajamas off and took off his rubber pants and took the pins out of his diaper and climbed out of the crib and put the diaper in the diaper pail and took a fresh diaper and climbed into the crib and put the diaper on Jacob and put in the pins and put on a fresh pair of rubber pants and Jacob said, "Dress me." So Mitzi lifted Jacob out of the crib

and put him on the floor and she put on his shirt and his overalls and his socks. She put on his right shoe and his left shoe and his snowsuit and his mittens and tied his hat under his chin and said, "*Now* let's go."

Jacob said, "In your pajamas?"

When Mitzi had got on her shirt and her skirt and her socks and her shoes and put herself into her snowsuit and found her mittens and tied her hat under her chin, Jacob said, "Now let's go."

Mitzi put Jacob in his stroller and pushed the stroller out of their front door and along the hall to the elevator.

"Only I can't reach the button," she said.

"Take me out and hold me up," said Jacob. So Mitzi took Jacob out of the stroller and held him way up and Jacob pressed the button. When the elevator came, Mitzi pushed the stroller in, the door closed and the elevator went down to the ground floor and the door opened.

The doorman in the lobby said, "Good morning, Mitzi. Good morning, Jacob."

Jacob said, "Dadadada."

Mitzi said, "We're going to Grandma and Grandpa's house."

The doorman helped Mitzi take the stroller down the steps and Mitzi pushed Jacob to the corner of the street and called, "TAXI!"

A taxi stopped and the driver got out and came around to their side. He lifted Jacob out of the stroller and put him in the back seat and lifted Mitzi in and folded up the stroller and put it in the empty front seat and walked around to his side and got in and said, "Where to?"

"Grandma and Grandpa's house, please," said Mitzi.

"Where do they live?" asked the driver.

"I don't know," said Mitzi.

So the driver got out and came around to the other side and took the stroller from the front seat and unfolded it on the sidewalk and took Jacob out and put him in the stroller and took Mitzi out and put her on the sidewalk and walked around to his side and got in and drove away.

Mitzi pushed Jacob back to the house.

The doorman helped her get the stroller up the stairs and he pushed the elevator button for them. They got out on their floor and went in their front door and into their room. Mitzi took Jacob out of the stroller and untied his hat and took off his mittens. She took off his snowsuit and his right shoe and his left shoe and his socks and his overalls and his shirt and put on his pajamas and lifted him into his crib. Then she undressed herself and put her pajamas on and got back into bed and covered herself up and then the alarm clock rang in her mother and father's room.

Mitzi's mother came into the children's room and said, "Good morning, Mitzi," and Mitzi said, "Morning, Mommy," and her mother said, "Good morning, Jacob," and Jacob said, "Dadada."

"Come to Mommy, Jacob," said his mother. "I'll get you a *nice* bottle and change your diaper," and she took him out of the crib and she said, "Mitzi, today can you be a *really big* girl and take off your *own* pajamas *all* by yourself?"

"You do it," said Mitzi. "I'm exhausted."

"Exhausted, are you!" said her mother. "How come you're exhausted so early in the morning?"

"Because I am," said Mitzi. "Mommy! Where do Grandma and Grandpa live?"

"Six West Seventy-seventh Street," said her mother. "Why do you ask?"

"Because," said Mitzi.

THE GIRL WITH THE GREEN EAR

written by Margaret Mahy
illustrated by Shirley Hughes

DON'T CUT THE LAWN!

Mr. Pomeroy went to his seaside cottage for the holidays. The sea was right, the sand was right, the sun was right, the salt was right. But outside his cottage the lawn had grown into a terrible tussocky tangle. Mr. Pomeroy decided that he would have to cut it.

He got out his lawn mower, Snapping Jack.

"Now for some fun!" said Snapping Jack. "Things have been very quiet lately. I've been wanting to get at that grass for weeks and weeks."

Mr. Pomeroy began pushing the lawn mower, and the grass flew up and out. However, he had gone only a few steps when out of the tangly, tussocky jungle flew a lark that cried:

> "Don't cut the lawn, don't cut the lawn!
> You will cut my little nestlings,
> which have just been born."

Mr. Pomeroy went to investigate, and there, sure enough, were four baby larks in a nest on the ground.

"No need to worry, madam!" cried Mr. Pomeroy to the anxious mother. "We will go around your nest and cut the lawn farther away."

So they went around the nest and started cutting the lawn farther away, with Snapping Jack snapping cheerfully. But at that moment out jumped a mother hare and cried:

> "Don't cut the lawn, don't cut the lawn!
> You will cut my little leveret,
> who has just been born."

Mr. Pomeroy went to investigate, and there, sure enough, was a little brown leveret, safe in his own little tussocky form.

"We'll have to go farther away to do our mowing," Mr. Pomeroy said to Snapping Jack. So they went farther away and Mr. Pomeroy said, "Now we'll really begin cutting this lawn."

"Right!" said Snapping Jack. "We'll have no mercy on it."

But they had only just begun to have no mercy on the lawn when a tabby cat leaped out of the tussocky tangle and mewed at them:

"Don't cut the lawn, don't cut the lawn!

You will cut my little kittens,

who have just been born."

Mr. Pomeroy went to investigate, and there, sure enough, were two stripy kittens in a little golden tussocky, tangly hollow.

"This place is more like a zoo than a lawn," grumbled Snapping Jack. "We'll go farther away this time, but you must promise to be hard-hearted or the lawn will get the better of us."

"All right! If it happens again I'll be very hard-hearted," promised Mr. Pomeroy.

They began to cut where the lawn was longest, lankiest, tangliest, and most terribly tough and tussocky.

"I'm not going to take any notice of any interruptions this time," Mr. Pomeroy said to himself firmly.

"We'll really get down to business," said Snapping Jack, beginning to champ with satisfaction.

Then something moved in the long, lank, tussocky tangle. Something slowly sat up and stared at them with jeweled eyes. It was a big mother dragon, as green as grass, as golden as a tussock. She looked at them and she hissed:

"Don't cut the lawn, don't cut the lawn!

You will cut my little dragon,

who has just been born."

There among the leathery scraps of the shell of the dragon's egg was a tiny dragon, as golden and glittering as a bejeweled evening bag. It blew out a tiny flame at them, just like a cigarette lighter.

"Isn't he clever for one so young!" exclaimed his loving mother. "Of course I can blow out a very big flame. I could burn all this lawn in one blast if I wanted to. I could easily scorch off your eyebrows."

"But that's against the law!" croaked the alarmed Mr. Pomeroy.

"Oh, I'm afraid that wouldn't stop me," said the dragon. "Not if I was upset about anything. And if you mowed my baby I'd be very upset. I'd probably breathe fire hot enough to melt a lawn mower!"

"What do *you* think?" Mr. Pomeroy asked Snapping Jack.

"Let's leave it until next week," said Snapping Jack hurriedly.

"We don't want to upset a loving mother, do we? Particularly one that breathes fire!"

So the lawn was left alone and Mr. Pomeroy sat on his veranda enjoying the sun, or swam in the sea enjoying the salt water, and day by day he watched the cottage lawn grow more tussocky and more tangly. Then one day out of the tussocks and tangles flew four baby larks that began learning how to soar and sing as larks do. And out of the tussocks and tangles came a little hare that frolicked and frisked as hares do. And out of the tussocks and tangles came two stripy kittens that pounced and bounced as kittens do. And then out of the tussocks and tangles came a little dragon with golden scales and eyes like stars, and it laid its shining head on Mr. Pomeroy's knee and told him some of the wonderful stories that only dragons know. Even Snapping Jack listened with interest.

"Fancy that!" he was heard to remark. "I'm glad I talked Mr. Pomeroy out of mowing the lawn. Who'd ever believe a tussocky, tangly lawn could be home to so many creatures. There's more to a lawn than mere grass, you know!"

And Mr. Pomeroy, the larks, the little hare, the kittens, and the little dragon all agreed with him.

ELLEN'S LION

written and illustrated by Crockett Johnson

A Selection of Three Stories

CONVERSATION AND SONG

Ellen sat on the footstool and looked down thoughtfully at the lion. He lay on his stomach on the floor at her feet.

"Whenever you and I have a conversation I do all the talking, don't I?" she said.

The lion remained silent.

"I never let you say a single word," Ellen said.

The lion did not say a word.

"The trouble with me is I talk too much," Ellen continued. "I haven't been very polite, I guess. I apologize."

"Oh, that's all right, Ellen," the lion said.

Ellen sprang to her feet and jumped up and down in delight.

"You talked!" she cried. "You said something!"

"It wasn't anything that important," said the lion. "And watch where you're jumping."

"It was the way you said it," said Ellen, sitting down again. "You have such a funny deep voice!"

"I think my voice sounds remarkably like yours," the lion said.

"No, it sounds very different," Ellen told him, speaking with her mouth pulled down at the corners and her chin pressed against her chest to lower her voice. "This is how you talk."

"I don't make a face like that," said the lion.

"You don't have to. Your face is always like that," Ellen said. "It's probably why you have the kind of voice you have."

The lion did not reply.

"I didn't mean to hurt your feelings," said Ellen.

"I'm nothing but a stuffed animal. I have no feelings," the lion said, and with a sniff, he became silent.

"I like your face the way it is," Ellen said, trying to think of a way to cheer him up. "And you have got a lovely deep voice. Let's sing a song."

"What song?" said the lion.

Ellen thought of a cheerful song.

"Let's sing 'Old King Cole.'"

The lion immediately began to sing.

"Old King Cole was a merry old soul—"

"Wait," Ellen said. "Let's sing it together."

"All right," said the lion.

"Old King Cole was a merry old soul—" Ellen sang, and then she stopped. "You're not singing."

"And a merry old soul was he—" sang the lion.

"—was he," sang Ellen, trying to catch up. *"He called for his pipe and he called for his bowl—"*

She realized the lion was not singing with her and she stopped again.

"And he called for his fiddlers three—" sang the lion.

"Can't we both sing at the same time?" Ellen said.

The lion considered the question.

"I don't think we can," he said. "Do you?"

"Let's talk," Ellen said. "It's easier."

"All right," said the lion.

"Think of something to talk about," Ellen said.

"All right," said the lion.

Ellen waited. After a minute or two she looked at the lion. He lay motionless on the floor.

"He thought so hard he fell asleep," she whispered as she left the playroom on tiptoe.

Two Pairs of Eyes

"I wish I had a drink of water," said Ellen in the middle of the night.

"Well, get one," said the lion, from the other end of the pillow.

"I'm afraid," Ellen said.

"Of what?" said the lion.

"Of things," said Ellen.

"What kind of things?" said the lion.

"Frightening things," Ellen said. "Things I can't see in the dark. They always follow along behind me."

"How do you know?" said the lion. "If you can't see them—"

"I can't see them because they're always behind me," said Ellen. "When I turn around they jump behind my back."

"Do you hear them?" asked the lion.

"They never make a sound," Ellen said, shivering. "That's the worst part of it."

The lion thought for a moment.

"Hmm," he said.

"They're awful," Ellen continued.

"Ellen," the lion said, "I don't think there are any such things."

"Oh, no? Then how can they scare me?" said Ellen indignantly. "They're terribly scary things."

"They must be exceedingly scary," said the lion. "If they keep hiding in back of you they can't be very brave."

Ellen frowned at the lion. Then she considered what he had said.

"I guess they're not very brave," she agreed. "They wouldn't dare bother me if I could look both ways at the same time."

"Yes," said the lion. "But who has two pairs of eyes?"

"Two people have," Ellen said, staring up at where the ceiling was when it wasn't so dark. "I wouldn't be afraid to go down the hall for a drink of water if I was two people."

Suddenly she reached out for the lion, dragged him to her, and looked him in the eyes.

"Mine are buttons," he said. "They're sewn on. I can't see very well in the dark."

"Nobody can," Ellen whispered as she got out of bed. "But the things don't know that."

"How do you know they don't know?" said the lion.

"I know all about them," said Ellen. "After all, I made them up in my head, didn't I?"

"Ah," said the lion. "I said there were no such things."

"But of course there are," Ellen said. "I just told you I made them up myself."

"Yes," the lion said. "But—"

"So I should know, shouldn't I?" said Ellen, putting the lion up on her shoulder so that he faced behind her. "Stop arguing with me and keep your eyes open."

"They're buttons," said the lion, bouncing on Ellen's shoulder as she walked across the bedroom. "My eyes never close."

"Good," said Ellen, and she opened the door to the hall.

With a firm grip on the lion's tail to hold him in place, she marched down the hall to the bathroom, drank a glass of water, and marched back to bed. She looked straight ahead all the way while the lion stared into the darkness behind her and during the entire trip not a single thing dared bother either of them.

Ellen came in with a brand-new squirrel, holding him high over her head.

"I just got him for my birthday," she said. "Isn't he adorable?"

"Is he?" the lion said.

Ellen cuddled the squirrel to her.

"Hasn't he got the most appealing expression?"

"Has he?" said the lion.

"And wait till you hear this," said Ellen, inserting a key in the squirrel's side and twisting it around and around. "Listen."

The squirrel began a song, but not at its proper beginning, and it came out of him in a tinkling voice that carried only the tune, not the words.

"—one horse open sleigh ay jingle bells jingle bells jingle all the way oh what fun it is to ride in a one horse open sleigh ay jingle bells—"

"Isn't he wonderful?" Ellen said.

"He has a music box inside of him," the lion said.

"I know," said Ellen, holding the squirrel against her cheek, listening to him, and stroking his fur. "That's what's so wonderful."

"Machinery," said the lion. "Just something to get out of order."

"You're jealous," Ellen said. "You haven't got a music box in your stomach."

"Neither have you," said the lion. "I don't think it is a matter to give either of us any great cause for envy."

"I swallowed a whistle once," said Ellen.

"I remember," the lion said. "And it was quite a calamity. The doctor came. Your mother and father and I were up all night."

"Were you here then?" Ellen said. "It was long ago. I was little."

"I was here long before that," said the lion. "Even before you had the measles. Remember? I stayed in bed with you the whole time."

"—sleigh ay jingle bells jingle bells jingle all the—"

The squirrel stopped tinkling. Ellen reached for the key and wound him up again while she stared at the lion.

"You might have caught the measles," she said.

"Your mother disinfected me," the lion said. "It took three days on the clothesline in the sun for me to dry. My fur faded."

"—way oh what fun it is to ride in a one horse open sleigh ay jingle bells—"

Ellen carried the squirrel, tinkling merrily again, to a corner of the room and set him on the floor.

"The lion and I are talking about things from long ago," she explained, leaving him and returning to the lion. "When you were disinfected it must have been as bad as the time we had to put you in the washing machine after you fell in the mixing bowl."

"It was much the same sort of experience," said the lion.

"I remember when we pulled you out of the brownie batter," said Ellen, suddenly laughing. "It was very funny."

"It's funny now," said the lion. "Looking back on it."

In the corner of the room the squirrel tinkled on.

"Remember when Sarge Thompson kidnapped you and took you to his kennel?" Ellen said.

"You cried," said the lion.

"But I rescued you," said Ellen.

"I was proud of you," said the lion.

"—bells jingle bells jingle all the way oh what—"

The squirrel tinkled to a stop. Nobody noticed. Nobody wound him up again. Ellen and the lion were busy talking over old times.

THE BEARS ON HEMLOCK MOUNTAIN

written by Alice Dalgliesh
illustrated by Helen Sewell

ABOUT JONATHAN

Jonathan lived in a gray stone farmhouse at the foot of Hemlock Mountain. Now Hemlock Mountain was not a mountain at all, it was a hill, and not a very big one. But someone had started calling it Hemlock Mountain, and the name had stuck. Now everyone talked about "going over Hemlock Mountain."

It was the year when Jonathan was eight that he went over Hemlock Mountain. He was a fine big boy for his age. That was why his mother could send him over the Mountain all by himself.

The winter had been a cold one. Even now, in early spring, there was snow on the ground. The birds and the squirrels and the rabbits had a hard time finding anything to eat, so every day Jonathan remembered to feed them. Jonathan loved animals and birds. He knew the tracks that each one made in the snow.

The small creatures could not find enough to eat, but it was not so with Jonathan's aunts and uncles and cousins. All they had to do was to come to the gray stone farmhouse and there was always plenty of food. Jonathan's mother was a fine cook and all the aunts, uncles and cousins knew it. They liked to drop in for supper and to sit around the table in front of the big fireplace.

Such good suppers! There would be roast chicken or roast duck or roast goose, brown and done to a turn. There would be potatoes and turnips, carrots and corn. And of course there would be pies—pumpkin and apple and squash. While for those who like cookies, there were crisp brown ones cut into every shape you can imagine.

Jonathan's mother liked company but sometimes—oh, once in a while—she wished they did not have so much of it. Or that the aunts and uncles and cousins were not quite so hungry.

YOUNG UNCLE JAMES

Jonathan was very fond of his uncles. He was fond of his cousins and his aunts. It was pretty fine for a boy to have so many uncles and aunts. If all his uncles and aunts stood side by side they would go all the way from the house to the gate—or very nearly.

He liked all the uncles, but best of all he liked young Uncle James. Young Uncle James was only fourteen years old, so he and Jonathan were friends.

Young Uncle James had eyes that saw and ears that heard.

"Look," he would say to Jonathan. "Down by that tree stump is a cottontail."

The Bears on Hemlock Mountain

 Then he and Jonathan were very still. They could see the little brown rabbit washing his face and his ears.

"Listen," young Uncle James would say. "There is a song sparrow. Do you hear what he says?"

Then he and Jonathan were very still. They could see the song sparrow singing on a branch. And the song sparrow was saying, over and over again,

"Put on the kettle, kettle, kettle!"

Once Jonathan and Uncle James went down to the brook. It was late in the day and the shadows were long.

"What are we going to see?" asked Jonathan.

"Wait and you will find out," said Uncle James.

So they waited and listened. It was hard for Jonathan to keep so still.

They waited and listened. And at last a raccoon came down to the brook. He had an apple in his mouth.

"Look!" said Uncle James. "Look carefully, Jonathan."

Jonathan looked. The raccoon took the apple in his two front paws. He dipped it in the water and dipped it and dipped it and dipped it again.

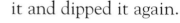"'Coons like their food wet," said Uncle James.

That was the way of it. Every day Jonathan and Uncle James listened and looked. They never threw sticks at the animals, or scared the birds. Soon all the animals and birds were their friends. The squirrel was the best friend of all. He came very near to get nuts from Jonathan.

"Uncle James," said Jonathan. "Did you ever see a bear?"

"Well, now," said Uncle James, looking important. "I believe I did. But it was years ago, Jonathan."

"How many years ago?"

"Before you were born. Yes, it was before you were born."

"I would like to see a bear," said Jonathan. "I would rather see a bear than anything in the world."

"Maybe you will!" said Uncle James.

That was all he said. But Jonathan kept on thinking about bears.

THE IRON POT

Now if there are lots of aunts and uncles there are likely to be lots of new cousins. Jonathan kept having new cousins all the time.

It happened that a new small cousin of Jonathan's was being christened. So, of course, all the aunts and uncles and older cousins were going to the christening. Afterwards, so they thought, it would be fine to have supper in the gray stone farmhouse.

It was fine when relatives came in ones and twos, or threes and fours, or even in fives and sixes. But this particular time twenty of them were coming.

"Twenty of them!" said Jonathan's mother.

"Whatever shall we do?"

"Give them a good, big, hearty stew," said Jonathan's father. "Fill 'em up with it and then give 'em cookies. That should be enough."

"It's a fine idea," said Jonathan's mother as she rolled out the cookie dough and cut it into stars and bells, hearts and flowers, rabbits and birds and a dozen other things.

"A fine idea. But where in all the world shall I get a pot big enough to make a stew for twenty—no, twenty-three—people? For of course you and Jonathan and I must be counted in."

"I should think so!" Jonathan's father said. "And remember I am very hungry in this cold weather."

He certainly was.

But then he was a big man and worked hard on the farm. Even in the wintertime he worked hard, for there were the cows to be milked and all the other animals to be fed. There was wood to be cut. This kept the big fire going so that Jonathan's mother could cook all the good things the family liked to eat. Jonathan helped carry in the wood.

Jonathan's mother kept thinking about the stew and about the pot that would be big enough to cook it.

"I know!" she said to Jonathan, as he brought in an armful of wood, "your aunt Emma, over across Hemlock Mountain, has the biggest iron pot you ever laid eyes on."

"*I* never laid eyes on it," said Jonathan.

"Then you are going to," said his mother. "Your father is much too busy to go for it, but you can go and fetch it."

"Me?" said Jonathan. "All alone? They say there are bears on Hemlock Mountain."

"Stuff and nonsense," said his mother. "Many's the time I've been over Hemlock Mountain and not a bear did I see. Your Uncle James must have been telling you stories. Besides if there *were* bears they'd be asleep this time of year. And besides there *are* no bears."

"But it's a long way and the pot is heavy," Jonathan said. "And bears wake up in the spring."

"You are a big boy, now," his mother told him. "Get on your warm coat and your warm cap and your warm muffler and go quickly, for you must be back before it is dark. Tomorrow, early, I shall start the stew."

So Jonathan put on his coat and his muffler and pulled his warm cap down over his ears. He filled his pockets full of nuts for the squirrels on Hemlock Mountain, and he took some bread crumbs for the birds.

Then Jonathan went tramping to the gate, his boots making big footprints in the snow. Crunch! Crunch! Crunch! Then suddenly he turned and went back.

"Ma," he said when his mother opened the door, "will you give me some carrots?"

"Some carrots? Whatever for?"

"For the rabbits on Hemlock Mountain. I have nuts for the squirrels, and bread crumbs for the birds. Now I want carrots for the rabbits."

"Well, of course," said his mother, and she gave him a bunch of carrots. Then she went to the cookie jar and brought out a handful of cookies.

"And these are for you," she said. "Just in case you should be late coming over the mountain. But you must not be late, for it still gets dark early."

"Thank you," said Jonathan, and he put the cookies in his pocket. "I won't be late, because

MAYBE

   THERE ARE BEARS

      ON HEMLOCK MOUNTAIN!"

Then he was off again, crunch, crunch, crunch in his big boots, making big footprints all the way to the gate.

The Bears on Hemlock Mountain

When Jonathan was out of sight of the house, his mother began to worry just a little bit about bears on Hemlock Mountain.

Stuff and nonsense, she said to herself. There *are* no bears on Hemlock Mountain. But perhaps . . . She went back to her cookie making and tried to forget about it.

But she couldn't forget. She found she was cutting out cookies to a kind of rhythm:

There   *are*   no   bears   on

Hemlock   Mountain

No   bears   at   all

Of   course   there   are   no

bears   on   Hemlock   Mountain

No bears, no bears, no bears, no bears at all.

Jonathan went up Hemlock Mountain eating a cookie as he went.

It was very still on Hemlock Mountain. The only sound was Jonathan's boots going crunch, crunch, crunch on the snow. He could look back and see the big footprints that he made. It was very lonely. So lonely that Jonathan made up words to go with the crunch, crunch of his boots. Strangely enough they were the same words as his mother's:

> THERE *are* NO BEARS
> > ON HEMLOCK MOUNTAIN,
> > > NO BEARS AT ALL.
> > OF COURSE THERE ARE NO BEARS
> > > ON HEMLOCK MOUNTAIN,
> > NO BEARS, NO BEARS, NO BEARS,
> > > NO BEARS AT ALL.

When he got to the top of Hemlock Mountain, Jonathan was out of breath. So he sat down on a log to rest. And as he rested he took out of his pocket the nuts and the carrots and the bread crumbs. He put them on the snow a little distance from where he was sitting.

It was very still and quiet. To keep up his courage Jonathan said to himself:

> THERE *are*
> > NO BEARS
> > > ON HEMLOCK MOUNTAIN,
> NO BEARS AT ALL.
> THERE ARE NO BEARS
> > ON HEMLOCK MOUNTAIN,
> NO BEARS, NO BEARS, NO BEARS,
> > NO BEARS
> > > AT ALL.

Then there began to be little sounds all around him. And out of the woods came rabbits, hopping over the snow. They came straight to the carrots Jonathan had brought for them.

Out of the woods came squirrels. They looked around with bright eyes, and put one paw on their hearts, the way squirrels do. Then they came straight to the nuts Jonathan had brought for them.

And then came the winter birds, hopping and twittering. They came straight to the bread crumbs Jonathan had brought for them.

The Bears on Hemlock Mountain

Jonathan sat as still as still. He was not lonely now. And he was not worried about bears. He had lots of company. For quite a long time he sat there watching the rabbits and the squirrels and the birds.

But time was going on and the sun was lower in the sky.

Jonathan knew he must be on his way. So he got to his feet, and his boots went crunch, crunch, crunch on the snow.

All the rabbits went hopping back to the woods. The squirrels looked around with their paws on their hearts. Then, whisk! and away up the trees. The birds flew up into the branches. Jonathan was alone.

Down Hemlock Mountain

Now Jonathan started down the other side of Hemlock Mountain. It was very still and his boots went crunch, crunch, crunch on the snow. Jonathan could look back and see the endless footprints he was making.

It was quiet, so quiet! To keep up his courage Jonathan said to himself, marking time to the sound of his steps on the snow:

> THERE *are* NO BEARS
>> ON HEMLOCK MOUNTAIN,
> NO BEARS, NO BEARS AT ALL.
> OF COURSE THERE ARE NO BEARS
>> ON HEMLOCK MOUNTAIN,
> NO BEARS, NO BEARS, NO BEARS, NO BEARS
>> AT ALL.

He went down the mountain much faster than he had come up. At the bottom he stopped and looked back at the enormous footprints he had made in the snow. There were no other footprints, not any at all. Jonathan had been the only one on Hemlock Mountain. It made him feel lonesome just to think of it.

And as Jonathan stood still, there was a strange, small sound. Drip, drip, drip! The sun was warm on the south side of the mountain and the snow and ice were beginning to melt. Drip, drip, drip from the branches of trees. Drip, drip, drip from the rocks.

It sounds like spring, Jonathan said to himself. *It feels like spring.* I HOPE THE BEARS DON'T KNOW IT!

Aunt Emma's House

When Jonathan began to think about spring and about bears, it made him feel the need to hurry.

So he went on, very quickly. Down here on the other side of Hemlock Mountain the sun was even warmer. Drip, drip, drip went the trees. Jonathan's boots no longer went crunch on the snow. They sank into it, and he made bigger footprints than before.

Soon he was at his Aunt Emma's house. By the gate some hungry birds were hopping about on the snow. Jonathan felt in his pockets. Yes, there were a few crumbs. So he threw them to the birds and went round to the back door.

Jonathan lifted the brass knocker and let it fall. How loud it sounded! But it was a cozy, comfortable sound, not a lonely one. Jonathan had come over Hemlock Mountain and here he was, safe at his aunt's house! He began to feel big and noble and brave. Jonathan seemed to grow an inch taller as he stood waiting for his aunt to open the door.

Footsteps came hurrying through the kitchen. The door opened and there was his Aunt Emma. She was wearing a big white apron, and

Jonathan hoped she had been cooking. By now he was very, very hungry.

"Mercy sakes, Jonathan!" said his Aunt Emma. "What are you doing here this snowy day? Come in!"

Jonathan went in, but first he shook the snow carefully off his boots. Aunt Emma was a good housekeeper. Then he went into the kitchen. A big fire was burning, and the kitchen was pleasant and warm. The air was full of a good smell. Jonathan sniffed—M-m-m- cookies!

It was quite hard to be polite. But Jonathan sat down in the rocker and tried not to look hungry. He had quite forgotten about the cookies eaten on the way.

"Well," said his Aunt Emma, "what brings you here?"

"I came to see you, Aunt," said Jonathan, full of politeness and hunger. The big black cat came and rubbed against his legs. Jonathan stroked her.

"Tush!" said his aunt. "You can't tell me that you came all the way over Hemlock Mountain just for a visit?" Then she looked at him sharply.

"Jonathan! *Did you come all alone over Hemlock Mountain?*"

"Yes," said Jonathan. "Why?"

"Because—" said his aunt.

"Because what?" asked Jonathan.

"Because, nothing." But Jonathan knew she was thinking about BEARS.

The cat arched her back and purred. Jonathan thought he had been polite long enough. So he allowed himself to give just a small sniff.

Sniff, sniff. "Smells good in here!" said Jonathan.

Sniff!

"Mercy's sake," said his aunt. "You must be hungry coming all the way over the Mountain. Would you like a cookie?"

"Please. Thank you," said Jonathan hoping he did not sound too eager. Hoping, too, that it would not be just *one* cookie.

He need not have worried. His aunt brought a plate with a whole pile of crisp crunchy cookies. She put them on the table beside him. Then she brought a mug and a big blue pitcher of milk.

Mm-m-m! The cookies were good! Not as good as his mother's perhaps, but *good*, just the same.

Jonathan rocked and munched on cookies. He drank milk. He rocked and munched and drank. The clock on the kitchen shelf did its best to tell him that time was passing.

"Tick-tock, tick-tock, time to go, tick-tock."

But Jonathan rocked and ate and did not hear it.

"Tick-tock, tick-tock."

The fire was warm and Jonathan was most awfully full. He stopped rocking and slowly, slowly, slowly, his eyes closed. Jonathan was asleep!

Mercy's sakes! thought his aunt. *I wonder what the boy wanted? But it would be a shame to wake him . . .* So she let him sleep.

Time went on. Jonathan slept. The sun went lower in the sky.

"Tick-tock!" said the clock. "Time to go!" But Jonathan went on sleeping.

The big black cat had also been sleeping by the fire. Now she got up, stretched, and came to rub against Jonathan's legs.

As she rubbed she purred, a loud rumble of a purr. And then, at last, Jonathan awoke!

At first he did not know where he was. Then he remembered.

"Oh!" he said. "It is late and Ma said I must be home before dark."

"There is still time, if you hurry," said his aunt. She wondered if Jonathan had come there just to eat her cookies. Why should he when his mother made such good cookies of her own. It was quite a puzzle.

Jonathan put on his muffler and his coat and his boots.

"Goodbye Aunt Emma," he said politely.

"Goodbye Jonathan. Do not waste time going over the mountain."

"Why not?"

"Because . . ."

"Because what?"

"Oh, just because . . ."

Jonathan was quite sure she was thinking about bears. But he was brave, and off he went toward Hemlock Mountain.

Jonathan had gone quite a way before it suddenly came to him. He stood still in the snow, feeling very cross with himself. You and I know what he had forgotten.

THE BIG IRON POT!

There was nothing for poor Jonathan to do but to turn and go back.

How silly I am, he said to himself. How silly I am!

In a short time he was back at his Aunt Emma's house. Once more he lifted the brass knocker. Aunt Emma came to the door.

"Jonathan! Did you forget something?"

"I forgot what I came for," Jonathan said truthfully. "Mom sent me to ask for the loan of your big iron pot. After the christening all the aunts and uncles and cousins are coming to supper."

"And as I am one of them, I'll be glad to lend you my big iron pot," said Aunt Emma. She went into the kitchen and came back with the big iron pot. It was very large. Now Jonathan did not feel as if he had grown at least an inch. He felt like a very small boy.

"Do you think you can carry it?"

"Indeed I can," said Jonathan, trying to feel big and brave again. He took the pot by the handle and started off toward Hemlock Mountain.

When he was out of sight his aunt began to worry.

"He is not very big," she told the black cat. "And it is growing dark."

"Purr-rr-rr," said the black cat. "Purr-rr-rr."

"Oh, don't tell *me*," said Jonathan's aunt with crossness in her voice. "YOU KNOW

THERE MAY BE BEARS

ON HEMLOCK MOUNTAIN!"

WATCH OUT, JONATHAN!

Jonathan and the big iron pot were going up the side of Hemlock Mountain.

Now it was really beginning to be dark. Jonathan knew he should hurry, but the iron pot was heavy. Jonathan's steps were heavy and slow. This time he was stepping in the big footprints he had made coming down.

It was really and truly dark. The tall trees were dark. The woods were dark and scary.

The Bears on Hemlock Mountain   193

"Crack!" a branch broke in the woods. It was as loud as a pistol shot.

"Woo-ooh. Woo-ooh!" That was an owl, but it was a most lonely sound.

Jonathan began to think about bears. And to keep up his courage he said, in time to his own slow steps:

THERE . . . ARE . . . NO . . . BEARS

            ON . . . HEMLOCK . . . MOUNTAIN

NO BEARS . . . NO . . . BEARS . . . AT . . . ALL.

He was tired and out of breath. So he rested for a minute, then he went on saying:

THERE . . . ARE . . . NO . . . BEARS . . .

          ON . . . HEMLOCK . . . MOUNTAIN.

NO BEARS . . .

Watch out, Jonathan. WATCH OUT! What was that, among the trees, right on top of the mountain? Two big, dark . . . what could they be?

They moved slowly . . . slowly . . . but they were coming nearer . . . and nearer . . . and nearer . . .

Jonathan had to think quickly. There was only one thing to be done. Jonathan did it. He put the big iron pot upside down on the snow. Then he dug out a place and crawled under it.

The pot was like a safe house. Jonathan dug out another little place in the snow so that he could breathe.

Then he waited.

PAWS ON THE SNOW

Crunch! Crunch! Crunch! It was the sound of big, heavy paws in the snow.

The bears were coming!

Crunch! Crunch! Crunch! Nearer and nearer and nearer . . .

Jonathan's hair stood up straight on his head. He thought about a lot of things. He thought of his mother and father and the gray stone farm-house. Had they missed him? Would they come to look for him? He thought about the bears and wondered how they knew it was spring.

Crunch! Crunch! Crunch! Nearer and nearer. . . Jonathan made fool-ish words to the sound just to keep up his courage:

THERE . . . ARE . . . NO . . . BEARS

    ON . . . HEMLOCK . . . MOUNTAIN . . .

NO . . . BEARS . . . AT . . . ALL . . .

But the sound had stopped. The bears were *right beside the big iron pot.* Jonathan could hear them breathing.

And he was all alone on Hemlock Mountain.

Suddenly, above the breathing of the bears, Jonathan heard a noise.

It was a twittering and a chattering. The twittering was the soft, com-fortable noise that birds make before they go to sleep.

And then Jonathan knew that the trees were full of birds and squir-rels. He was not alone on Hemlock Mountain.

Perhaps the bears knew this, too. Perhaps they had not quite waked up from their long winter nap. They sat there by the big iron pot. They waited and waited. But they did not try to dig under it.

Inside the iron pot it was dark. Jonathan was far from comfortable.

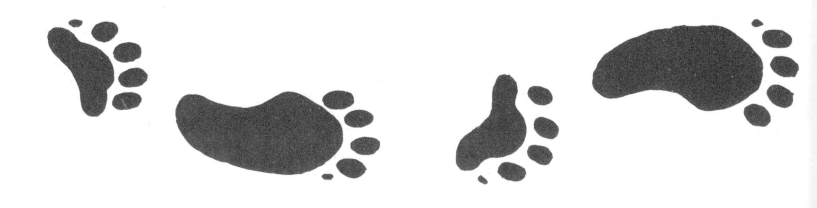

Outside he could hear the bears going sniff, sniff, sniff. Poor Jonathan!

Oh, he said to himself. *Why did I wait so long at Aunt Emma's? Why did I eat so many cookies? Why did I go to sleep?* There did not seem to be any answer to these questions, so he stopped asking them.

The birds kept up their twittering and the squirrels kept up their chattering.

Sniff, sniff went the bears. One began scraping at the snow around the iron pot.

Poor Jonathan!

Then the birds stopped twittering and the squirrels stopped chattering. The bears stopped sniffing and listened. What was that?

Crunch! Crunch! Crunch!

Away off in the distance there was the sound of boots on the snow. Someone was coming up Hemlock Mountain!

It was very still. The only sound was the crunch of boots. And at last Jonathan heard it. His father's voice!

"Hello-o-o-oh, Jon-a-than!"

"Hello-o-o-oh, Pa!"

Jonathan's voice did not sound very loud under the iron pot. Would his father hear it?

Again his father's voice came, nearer and louder.

"HELLO-O-O-OH, JON-A-THAN!"

"HELLO-O-O-OH, PA!"

The bears had had enough of this. They went lumbering off into the woods. And the crunch of boots on the snow came nearer and nearer . . .

THERE ARE BEARS

Jonathan pushed back the big iron pot and stood up.

There were no bears. But up the path came his father, carrying his gun. And with him were Jonathan's Uncle James and his Uncle Samuel, his Uncle John and his Uncle Peter. Jonathan had never in all his life been so glad to see the uncles.

"Jonathan!" said his father, "what a fright you have given us! Where have you been all this time?"

"Coming over Hemlock Mountain," said Jonathan in a small voice. And he ran right into his father's arms.

"Well," said his father, when he had finished hugging Jonathan. "What is this?" He was looking at the big iron pot. "And why is it upside down?"

"Bears," said Jonathan.

"THERE

    are

       BEARS ON HEMLOCK MOUNTAIN."

"Stuff and nonsense!" said his father.

"But you are carrying your gun," said Jonathan. "So is uncle . . ."

"Well . . ." said his father.

Jonathan pointed to the bear tracks in the snow.

"Bears," he said firmly.

"THERE *are*

      BEARS ON HEMLOCK MOUNTAIN."

Jonathan's father looked at the bear tracks in the snow. His uncles looked at them, too.

"So!" they said. "So-o-o!"

And the uncles went off into the woods with their guns.

"You and I must go home, Jonathan," said his father. "Your mother is worrying herself sick. You have been a mighty long time coming over Hemlock Mountain."

"Yes, Pop," said Jonathan, and he hung his head.

"But what kept you so long?" asked his father. They were going down the mountain, now, and Jonathan's father was carrying the big iron pot.

"Well," said Jonathan. "First I ate cookies, then I drank milk, then I slept . . ."

"H'm," said his father. "It is not the way to do when you are sent on an errand. But I guess you have learned that by this time."

It was very still on Hemlock Mountain.

There was only the crunch, crunch of boots on the snow. A squirrel scampered to a tree. He sat looking at Jonathan and his father, his paws on his heart.

"I know what I know!" he seemed to say.

Crack! What was that? A shot in the woods? Or a branch snapping? The squirrel, frightened, scampered higher up in the tree.

"Oh!" said Jonathan.

"Something tells me," his father said. "Something tells me we shall have bear steak for dinner!"

They kept on down the mountain. The birds twittered in the trees.

"We know what we know."

"The birds and the squirrels and the rabbits helped me," Jonathan said. "They are my friends."

"How could they help you?" asked his father. "They are so little."

"Well . . ." said Jonathan. But now they were near the gray stone farmhouse and there was no time to explain.

The firelight shone through the open door. It made a warm, golden path on the snow. And in the doorway was Jonathan's mother.

"Oh, Jonny!" she said, as she hugged him. "How glad I am that you are safely home!"

As for Jonathan, all he said in a rather out-of-breath way was:

"THERE . . . *are* . . . BEARS

       ON . . . HEMLOCK . . . MOUNTAIN,

THERE . . .

       ARE . . .

          BEARS!"

Then he took the iron pot from his father and set it down in the middle of the floor. Now his voice was proud.

"I brought it," he said. "All the way over Hemlock Mountain. And here it is!"

THE TRUE STORY OF THE 3 LITTLE PIGS

as told to Jon Scieszka
illustrated by Lane Smith

Everybody knows the story of the Three Little Pigs. Or at least they think they do. But I'll let you in on a little secret. Nobody knows the real story, because nobody has ever heard *my* side of the story.

I'm the wolf. Alexander T. Wolf. You can call me Al.

I don't know how this whole Big Bad Wolf thing got started, but it's all wrong.

Maybe it's because of our diet.

Hey, it's not my fault wolves eat cute little animals like bunnies and sheep and pigs. That's just the way we are. If cheeseburgers were cute, folks would probably think you were Big and Bad, too.

But like I was saying, the whole Big Bad Wolf thing is all wrong. The real story is about a sneeze and a cup of sugar.

This is the real story.

Way back in Once Upon a Time time, I was making a birthday cake for my dear old granny.

I had a terrible sneezing cold.

I ran out of sugar.

So I walked down the street to ask my neighbor for a cup of sugar.

Now this neighbor was a pig.

And he wasn't too bright, either.

He had built his whole house out of straw.

Can you believe it? I mean who in his right mind would build a house of straw?

So of course the minute I knocked on the door, it fell right in. I didn't want to just walk into someone else's house. So I called, "Little Pig, Little Pig, are you in?" No answer.

I was just about to go home without the cup of sugar for my dear old granny's birthday cake.

That's when my nose started to itch.

I felt a sneeze coming on.

Well I huffed.

And I snuffed.

And I sneezed a great sneeze.

And you know what? That whole darn straw house fell down. And right in the middle of the pile of straw was the First Little Pig—dead as a doornail.

He had been home the whole time.

It seemed like a shame to leave a perfectly good ham dinner lying there in the straw. So I ate it up.

Think of it as a big cheeseburger just lying there.

I was feeling a little bit better. But I still didn't have my cup of sugar.
So I went to the next neighbor's house.

This neighbor was the First Little Pig's brother.

He was a little smarter, but not much.

He had built his house of sticks.

I rang the bell on the stick house.

Nobody answered.

I called, "Mr. Pig, Mr. Pig, are you in?"

He yelled back, "Go away Wolf. You can't come in. I'm shaving the hairs on my chinny chin chin."

I had just grabbed the doorknob when I felt another sneeze coming on.

I huffed. And I snuffed. And I tried to cover my mouth, but I sneezed a great sneeze.

And you're not going to believe it, but this guy's house fell down just like his brother's.

When the dust cleared, there was the Second Little Pig—dead as a doornail. Wolf's honor.

Now you know food will spoil if you just leave it out in the open. So I did the only thing there was to do. I had dinner again. Think of it as a second helping. I was getting awfully full. But my cold was feeling a little better. And I still didn't have that cup of sugar for my dear old granny's birthday cake. So I went to the next house. This guy was the First and Second Little Pigs' brother. He must have been the brains of the family. He had built his house of bricks.

I knocked on the brick house. No answer.

I called, "Mr. Pig, Mr. Pig, are you in?"

And do you know what that rude little porker answered?

"Get out of here, Wolf. Don't bother me again."

Talk about impolite!

He probably had a whole sackful of sugar.

And he wouldn't give me even one little cup for my dear sweet old granny's birthday cake.

What a pig!

I was just about to go home and maybe make a nice birthday card instead of a cake, when I felt my cold coming on.

I huffed.

And I snuffed.

And I sneezed once again.

Then the Third Little Pig yelled, "And your old granny can sit on a pin!"

Now I'm usually a pretty calm fellow. But when somebody talks about my granny like that, I go a little crazy.

When the cops drove up, of course I was trying to break down this Pig's door. And the whole time I was huffing and puffing and sneezing and making a real scene.

The rest, as they say, is history.

The news reporters found out about the two pigs I had for dinner. They figured a sick guy going to borrow a cup of sugar didn't sound very exciting. So they jazzed up the story with all of that "Huff and puff and blow your house down." And they made me the Big Bad Wolf.

That's it.

The real story. I was framed.

But maybe you could loan me a cup of sugar.

NO KISS FOR MOTHER

written and illustrated by Tomi Ungerer

CHAPTER ONE

It is early in the morning. In his warm and cozy bed, sunk in a sound-proof slumber, Piper Paw dreams of chasing mice in a pastry shop.

His alarm clock has not gone off, because late last night, Piper took it apart. He wanted to find out what seconds, minutes, and hours looked like.

"That clock is full of them," he thought. "I can hear them ticking and tacking. I must see how they do it."

So he grabbed his flashlight, sneaked into the kitchen, and fetched his mother's can opener. With the opener he cut along the clock's rim and pried it open with a fork. The spring shot out with a snap and coiled itself around the curious kitten's nose.

In a rage, Piper dumped the lifeless shell of the clock out of the window, along with the flashlight and can opener. The missiles crashed seven floors below.

"That will teach it," he grumbled.

And now it is morning and time to wake up. But Piper's mother, Mrs. Velvet Paw, needs no alarm clock. She gets up every day at the same time, except on Sunday mornings, when they all brunch in bed.

"My, my, that Piper is still asleep," she says. "He'll be late for breakfast. I'd better go and wake my sweet little nestling up."

So she tippy-toes into her son's room.

"Time to get up," says Mother Paw. Piper does not hear. In his dream he has just cornered a purple mouse between two wedding cakes.

"Time to get up, Honey Pie," calls Mother Paw as she bends down to wedge a kiss in Sonny's ear.

And THAT wakes Piper up. Piper hates to be kissed, and to be kissed out of such a captivating dream is just about the most annoying thing in the world. With a hiss and a screech he jumps out of bed and shoots off, growling, to the bathroom.

Piper does not wash because he does not like to. He does not like to brush his teeth either. When he reaches the bathroom, he promptly latches the door to keep his mother out. He turns on the water, lets it run, and wets his washcloth. Then he rubs his toothbrush on the edge of the sink. "In case Mother Snoop is listening," Piper says.

Then he takes it easy for a while, looking at some soggy comic books which he keeps behind the tub.

Meanwhile, in Piper's room, Mother Paw has neatly laid out his clothing, cleaned and pressed the night before.

Piper does not like that either. He would rather choose his own outfit. "I look like a mail-order dummy," Piper complains, "neat and cute and tidy like a good little postcard pussy."

And every morning, with renewed rage, he crumples and rumples his clothes behind his mother's back.

"Breakfast is ready, darling," calls a motherly voice for the eighth or ninth time. Father Paw is already seated, and that can mean trouble.

"Come and sit down, my darling sweet," says Mrs. Paw. "Have some of this mice mush, my darling. Here, have some herring scraps and fried finch gizzards. I made them especially for you, my darling."

"Don't you *darling* me, Mother. It kills my appetite," snaps Piper. "I am no Honey Pie either. They'd throw me off the ball team if I played like a darling or looked like a Honey Pie, and, furthermore, you should be informed, sweet Mother Pie, that there is no such thing as a Honey Pie. I checked with Mr. Marzipan, the baker, who is an authority on confections, and he confirmed my suspicions. There is no such thing as a Honey Pie."

"You just enjoy hurting my feelings," Mother Paw says between sniffles. "Someday, when I am gone for good, you will miss my little dishes. Who knows? You'll end up alone in this world with no one to hug and love you, no one to prepare your meals and clean up your mess."

"That will suit me just fine," snickers Piper. "I am no baby, and I'll gladly do without any gooey attentions."

Mother Paw is on the verge of tears. "Stop talking to me that way,"

she moans. "Each word is a nail in my coffin. When I think of all the poor kittens in this world, starving, freezing in forsaken back alleys, my heart wrinkles with sorrow."

Father Paw does not say much. Most of the time he does not talk at all, especially at mealtime when he'd rather chew on food than words. "Enough is enough, and cut the nonsense," he orders Piper. "Not another word from you. There is such a thing as spanking, and you should know it, Mister Smart. If you have any doubts you can check it with my cane, who is an authority on corrections."

There is silence around the breakfast table now. Piper, his ears flattened, hides his muzzle in his bowl. "Time to go," says Mr. Paw, who works as supervisor in a rat-processing plant. "Skip the bus, Piper. I'll drive you to school today."

Father and son get up and slip on their overcoats. Mother kisses her boy good-bye. He makes a face and wipes off his jowls. "Are you not going to kiss your mother good-bye?" asks his father.

"No, not unless it's an emergency," replies Piper.

They take the elevator and emerge in the street. At the sight of his car, Mr. Paw's eyes turn red with rage. The windshield is cracked! "My car, my only car," he gasps. "Look at what the lousy punks have done to it. Look at that!" he goes on, pointing to an object lying in the gutter. "They tried to break into the car with a can opener."

Piper says nothing as he climbs into the car. He has not done his homework. He can't even skip school, now that his father is driving him there. "What is all this fussing with your mother lately?" asks Father Paw after a few blocks.

"She treats me like an infant," says Piper. "She embarrasses me and drives me up the wall, out of my blooming mind. She'd have me wear diapers if she could."

"Some mothers are made that way," explains Father Paw. "They can't help it. My mother was that way. So was my father's mother. Still, you should be nice to her. By the way, any time you want me to build some bookshelves in the bathroom, let me know. No sense letting your literature mildew under the tub. When I was your age I acted just like you. Never brushed my teeth. Ha ha! I fooled everyone by rubbing my toothbrush on the edge of the sink. Fooled everyone but the dentist. You can still hear the echo in my cavities. Well, here we are, son. Don't kiss me. Have a good day."

Piper steps out and waves good-bye to his father. There is no fooling the old cat. Besides, Piper really feels bad about the windshield.

CHAPTER TWO

In school, Piper is known as a rowdy. He is the troublemaker of his class. He is very ingenious when it comes to practical jokes. He sprinkles itching powder or catnip on everyone, stuffs the teacher's handbag with live spiders (big black ones), and pours airplane glue down the girls' necks. His locker is an arsenal of contraband firecrackers, noisemakers, smoke bombs, booby traps, peashooters—in short, anything that comes in handy to disrupt his class.

Yet his grades are good, for Piper has been blessed with an active brain. When Piper has not bothered with his homework (which is most of the time), he usually manages to get himself kicked out of class before homework inspection.

"It's better to have bad grades in conduct than in work," he tells the other pupils. For today, Piper had planned to let off a stink bomb. But the conversation with his father and the cracked windshield have sobered him down.

So meek, so well behaved is he that his teacher, Miss Purrypot, asks, "Is anything ailing our jester? Piper, you may be excused to see the nurse if you find it necessary." But Piper listlessly shakes his head.

At recess Piper's friends gang around him.

"You all right?"

"You sick or something?"

"What's up? Tell us," they all ask.

"I've got a hangover from too much kissing," he admits.

"Kissing?"

"Who is she?"

"You must be kidding."

"Is it Looloobah?"

"Is it Mitzy Bodyheat?"

"Or Miss Purrypot?" And that brings down a gale of laughter.

"Who knows?" adds Jefferson, the bully of the class. "It might have been the principal."

Piper can bear no more. He hits Jefferson in the left eye and catches him with an uppercut under the chin.

In a split and a slit of a second, both cats are rolling on the ground, hissing, hitting, biting and clawing, to the delight of the young specta-

tors, who are taking sides and making bets.

"Go on, Jeffy, kiss him one."

"Sock him, Piper, below the belt."

It is a rainy day, and both fighters turn into one ball of mud. By the time recess is over, the two cats are hardly recognizable. Jefferson's left eye is swollen shut and Piper's left ear is half torn off. He is bleeding like a fountain.

"It seems our head clown has one ear left to listen to my advice, which is: Go to the infirmary at once," exclaims Miss Purrypot as she sights the bleeding warriors. "And you, Jefferson, will escort him there."

The two boys leave without a word. "You look a mess. Have a cigar—you'll need it," says Jefferson as he pulls out a cigar butt and a lighter. "It's a corona, fresh. I picked it up in front of the opera house last night."

The boys, friends again, disappear in the bathroom to gather courage in a cloud of smoke.

The trip to the infirmary turns out to be a punishment of its own. Piper's ear has to be stitched back into place. The nurse, Miss Clot, does not have what is called a gentle touch (like Mother's). She prefers iodine to Mercurochrome, and that, holy mackerel, really, really hurts.

"I know your kind, you scoundrel," says the nurse as she threads the biggest needle she can find. "I know it was you who put a garter snake in my medicine cabinet, you worthless imp. Next time, I shall have the pleasure of clipping your ear altogether."

Yowls of pain drown her words. When the stitching is over, Miss Clot wraps up Piper's head in a huge bandage. "Well, Piper, with a red ribbon and a twig of holly you'd look like a regular Christmas present," snickers the nurse as the two boys walk away.

"I say that Clot woman is downright vicious," says Jefferson compassionately. "You should tell your mother about it."

"My mother!" says Piper. "She would make such a fuss, you have no idea. That would be even worse than all the pains in the world. I just hope nobody heard me cry."

CHAPTER THREE

Today is Mrs. Velvet Paw's shopping day. "I shall pick up my son at school and take him out for lunch," thinks Mrs. Paw as she gets ready. "There is casserole of mole innards on the menu at Zeldina's today, my sweet Piper's favorite dish."

Mrs. Paw loves to take her son out and show him off. Zeldina's restaurant is the best in town, and there Piper gets all the attention and helpings that befit Mother's young prince.

Velvet Paw and Zeldina are good friends. They play canasta on Wednesday nights and belong to the same bingo and bowling club.

Now it is noon. Mrs. Paw eagerly waits for her son to come out. She wears her cerise dress with matching hat and bag. Cerise is Piper's favorite color. The bell is ringing, and the school disgorges its flow of screaming pupils. Mrs. Paw searches for her son in the living rush. A bandaged head emerges.

"Piper! My son, my Piper!" she cries.

The sight of her wounded son has left Mrs. Paw breathless. Shaking, blind with tears, she snatches him out of the crowd and carries him off in a torrent of kisses. "My little sugar tiger, what have they done to you? Quick, a doctor! To the hospital," she cries. "Taxi, here, taxi."

Piper is mortified. He yanks himself free, screaming:
"Don't kiss me in front of people.
Kisses, kisses all the time.
I don't like it. I don't want it.
GOOD-MORNING KISSES,
GOOD-EVENING KISSES,
THANK-YOU KISSES,
KISS-ME KISSES,
SORRY-DARLING KISSES,
SUMMER KISSES,
WINTER KISSES,
LICKY KISSES,
SLOPPY KISSES
SOGGY KISSES."

And Piper goes on right there on the sidewalk.

Mother Paw does not know what to say, what to do. For once she wishes she were a mouse to crawl into the nearest crevice and hide. The taxi Mrs. Paw has hailed is waiting at the curb. "That's no way to talk to your mother," says the driver. "You should be ashamed of yourself."

"Yes, that's right!" Mrs. Paw exclaims. In an explosion of sudden anger, she steps forward and *slam-whack* she slaps her son into silence. She orders Piper into the taxi and gives the driver Zeldina's address.

Piper has never been hit by his mother before. Glum mother, sullen son drive away.

The lunch at Zeldina's seems endless and tasteless. Both are sorry for what has happened. Neither can find any words. There is nothing they can say. Piper hardly touches his casserole of mole innards. Mrs. Paw orders only a cup of tea. When it is time to return to school, Piper gets up and goes out of the restaurant without taking leave.

At school, no one mentions the events. But for his aching ear, it seems nothing has happened. At afternoon recess, Piper goes to his locker and brings out two stink bombs, a high-velocity slingshot, and an assortment of firecrackers.

Then he calls his pals over and says, "I need money. It's all for sale." The transaction takes place quickly. Firecrackers are hard to come by, and no one can manufacture stink bombs like Piper's.

Fifteen minutes before the end of school, Piper raises his hand. "Miss Purrypot, can I be excused?"

"In your case, yes," answers the teacher. "And I hope you will feel better tomorrow."

Piper runs down to a flower shop four blocks away. "I want some of those yellow roses," points out Piper as he puts all his change on the counter.

He gets back in time to catch the bus, his roses safely concealed under his coat.

At home Piper finds his mother busy scaling sardines at the kitchen table. "Hello, Piper," she volunteers with an attempt at a smile.

"Hello," replies Piper. He pulls out the bouquet and lays it down on the table, in front of his mother.

"Oh, how lovely," she exclaims. "What a surprise. Are they for me?"

"Yes, if you don't kiss me thank-you," says Piper.

"If you insist, I'll try," promises Mother Paw, smiling.

"Please do," says Piper, smiling back.

NO KISS FOR SON.

NO KISS FOR MOTHER.

THE PRACTICAL PRINCESS

written by Jay Williams
illustrated by Friso Henstra

Princess Bedelia was as lovely as the moon shining upon a lake full of waterlilies. She was as graceful as a cat leaping. And she was also extremely practical.

When she was born, three fairies had come to her cradle to give her gifts as was usual in that country. The first fairy had given her beauty. The second had given her grace. But the third, who was a wise old creature, had said, "I give her common sense."

"I don't think much of that gift," said King Ludwig, raising his eyebrows. "What good is common sense to a princess? All she needs is charm."

Nevertheless, when Bedelia was eighteen years old, something happened which made the king change his mind.

A dragon moved into the neighborhood. He settled in a dark cave on top of a mountain, and the first thing he did was to send a message to the king. "I must have a princess to devour," the message said, "or I shall breathe out my fiery breath and destroy the kingdom."

Sadly, King Ludwig called together his councillors and read them the message.

"Perhaps," said the Prime Minister, "we had better advertise for a knight to slay the dragon. That is what is generally done in these cases."

"I'm afraid we haven't time," answered the king. "The dragon has only given us until tomorrow morning. There is no help for it. We shall have to send him the princess."

Princess Bedelia had come to the meeting because, as she said, she liked to mind her own business and this was certainly her business.

"Rubbish!" she said. "Dragons can't tell the difference between princesses and anyone else. Use your common sense. He's just asking for me because he's a snob."

"That may be so," said her father, "but if we don't send you along, he'll destroy the kingdom."

"Right!" said Bedelia. "I see I'll have to deal with this myself." She left the council chamber. She got the largest and gaudiest of her state robes and stuffed it with straw, and tied it together with string. Into the center of the bundle she packed about a hundred pounds of gunpowder. She got two strong young men to carry it up the mountain for her. She stood in front of the dragon's cave and called, "Come out! Here's the princess!"

The dragon came blinking and peering out of the darkness. Seeing the bright robe covered with gold and silver embroidery, and hearing Bedelia's voice, he opened his mouth wide.

At once, at Bedelia's signal, the two young men swung the robe and gave it a good heave, right down the dragon's throat. Bedelia threw herself flat on the ground, and the two young men ran.

As the gunpowder met the flames inside the dragon, there was a tremendous explosion.

Bedelia got up, dusting herself off. "Dragons," she said, "are not very bright."

She left the two young men sweeping up the pieces, and she went back to the castle to have her geography lesson.

The lesson that morning was local geography. "Our kingdom, Arapathia, is bounded on the north by Istven," said the teacher. "Lord Garp, the ruler of Istven, is old, crafty, rich, and greedy."

At that very moment, Lord Garp of Istven was arriving at the castle. Word of Bedelia's destruction of the dragon had reached him. "That girl," said he, "is just the wife for me." And he had come with a hundred finely-dressed courtiers and many presents to ask King Ludwig for her hand.

The king sent for Bedelia. "My dear," he said, clearing his throat nervously, "just see who is here."

"I see. It's Lord Garp," said Bedelia. She turned to go.

"He wants to marry you," said the king.

Bedelia looked at Lord Garp. His face was like an old napkin, crumpled and wrinkled. It was covered with warts, as if someone had left crumbs on the napkin. He had only two teeth. Six long hairs grew from his chin, and none on his head. She felt like screaming.

However, she said, "I'm very flattered. Thank you, Lord Garp. Just let me talk to my father in private for a minute." When they had retired to a small room behind the throne, Bedelia said to the king, "What will Lord Garp do if I refuse to marry him?"

"He is rich, greedy, and crafty," said the king, unhappily. "He is also used to having his own way in everything. He will be insulted. He will probably declare war on us, and then there will be trouble."

"Very well," said Bedelia. "We must be practical."

She returned to the throne room. Smiling sweetly at Lord Garp, she said, "My lord, as you know, it is customary for a princess to set tasks for anyone who wishes to marry her. Surely, you wouldn't like me to break the custom. And you are bold and powerful enough, I know, to perform any task."

"That is true," said Lord Garp, smugly, stroking the six hairs on his chin. "Name your task."

The Practical Princess

"Bring me," said Bedelia, "a branch from the Jewel Tree of Paxis."

Lord Garp bowed, and off he went. "I think," said Bedelia to her father, "that we have seen the last of him. For Paxis is a thousand miles away, and the Jewel Tree is guarded by lions, serpents, and wolves."

But in two weeks, Lord Garp was back. With him he bore a chest, and from the chest he took a wonderful twig. Its bark was of rough gold. The leaves that grew from it were of fine silver. The twig was covered with blossoms, and each blossom had petals of mother-of-pearl and centers of sapphires, the color of the evening sky.

Bedelia's heart sank as she took the twig. But then she said to herself, "Use your common sense, my girl! Lord Garp never traveled two thousand miles in two weeks, nor is he the man to fight his way through lions, serpents, and wolves."

She looked more carefully at the branch. Then she said, "My lord, you know that the Jewel Tree of Paxis is a living tree, although it is all made of jewels."

"Why, of course," said Lord Garp. "Everyone knows that."

"Well," said Bedelia, "then why is it that these blossoms have no scent?"

Lord Garp turned red.

"I think," Bedelia went on, "that this branch was made by the jewelers of Istven, who are the best in the world. Not very nice of you, my lord. Some people might even call it cheating."

Lord Garp shrugged. He was too old and rich to feel

222

ashamed. But like many men used to having their own way, the more Bedelia refused him, the more he was determined to have her. "Never mind all that," he said. "Set me another task. This time, I swear I will perform it."

Bedelia sighed. "Very well. Then bring me a cloak made from the skins of the salamanders who live in the Volcano of Scoria."

Lord Garp bowed, and off he went. "The Volcano of Scoria," said Bedelia to her father, "is covered with red-hot lava. It burns steadily with great flames, and pours out poisonous smoke so that no one can come within a mile of it."

"You have certainly profited by your geography lessons," said the king, with admiration.

Nevertheless, in a week, Lord Garp was back. This time, he carried a cloak that shone and rippled with all the colors of fire. It was made of scaly skins, stitched together with fine golden wire. Each scale was red and orange and blue, like a tiny flame. Bedelia took the splendid cloak. She said to herself, "Use your head, miss! Lord Garp never climbed the red-hot slopes of the Volcano of Scoria."

A fire was burning in the fireplace of the throne room. Bedelia hurled the cloak into it. The skins blazed up in a flash, blackened, and fell to ashes.

Lord Garp's mouth fell open. Before he could speak, Bedelia said, "That cloak was a fake, my lord. The skins of salamanders who live in the Volcano of Scoria wouldn't burn in a little fire like that one."

Lord Garp turned pale with anger. He hopped up and down, unable at first to do anything but splutter.

"Ub—ub—ub!" he cried. Then, controlling himself, he said, "So be it. If I can't have you, no one shall!"

He pointed a long, skinny finger at her. On the finger was a magic ring.

The Practical Princess

At once, a great wind arose. It blew through the throne room. It sent King Ludwig flying one way and his guards the other. Bedelia was picked up and whisked off through the air. When she could catch her breath and look about her, she found herself in a room at the top of a tower.

Bedelia peered out of the window. About the tower stretched an empty, barren plain. As she watched, a speck appeared in the distance. A plume of dust rose behind it. It drew nearer and became Lord Garp on horseback.

He rode to the tower and looked up at Bedelia. "Aha!" he croaked. "So you are safe and snug, are you? And will you marry me now?"

"Never," said Bedelia, firmly.

"Then stay there until never comes," snarled Lord Garp.

Away he rode.

For the next two days, Bedelia felt very sorry for herself. She sat wistfully by the window, looking out at the empty plain. When she was hungry, food appeared on the table. When she was tired, she lay down on the narrow cot and slept. Each day, Lord Garp rode by and asked if she had changed her mind, and each day she refused him. Her only hope was that, as so often happens in old tales, a prince might come riding by who would rescue her.

But on the third day, she gave herself a shake.

"Now, then, pull yourself together," she said, sternly. "If you sit waiting for a prince to rescue you, you may sit here forever. Be practical! If there's any rescuing to be done, you're going to have to do it yourself."

She jumped up. There was something she had not yet done, and now she did it. She tried the door.

It opened.

Outside were three other doors. But there was no sign of a stair, or any way down from the top of the tower.

She opened two of the doors and found that they led into cells just like hers, but empty. Behind the fourth door, however, lay what appeared to be a haystack.

From beneath it came the sound of snores. And between snores, a voice said, "Six million and twelve . . . *snore* . . . six million and thirteen . . . *snore* . . . six million and fourteen . . ."

Cautiously, she went closer. Then she saw that what she had taken for a haystack was in fact an immense pile of blond hair. Parting it, she found a young man, sound asleep.

As she stared, he opened his eyes. He blinked at her. "Who—?" he said. Then he said, "Six million and fifteen," closed his eyes, and fell asleep again.

Bedelia took him by the shoulder and shook him hard. He awoke, yawning, and tried to sit up. But the mass of hair made this difficult.

"What on earth is the matter with you?" Bedelia asked. "Who are you?"

"I am Prince Perian," he replied, "the rightful ruler of—oh, dear, here I go again. Six million and . . ." His eyes began to close.

Bedelia shook him again. He made a violent effort and managed to wake up enough to continue, "—of Istven. But Lord Garp has put me under a spell. I have to count sheep jumping over a fence, and this puts me to slee—ee—ee—"

He began to snore lightly.

"Dear me," said Bedelia. "I must do something."

She thought hard. Then she pinched Perian's ear, and this woke him with a start.

"Listen," she said. "It's quite simple. It's all in your mind, you see. You are imagining the sheep jumping over the fence—No! Don't go to sleep again!

"This is what you must do. Imagine them jumping backwards. As you do, *count* them backwards, and when you get to *one*, you'll be wide awake."

The prince's eyes snapped open. "Marvelous!" he said. "Will it work?"

"It's bound to," said Bedelia. "If the sheep going one way will put you to sleep, their going back again will wake you up."

Hastily, the prince began to count, "Six million and fourteen, six million and thirteen, six million and twelve . . ."

"Oh, my goodness," cried Bedelia, "count by hundreds, or you'll never get there."

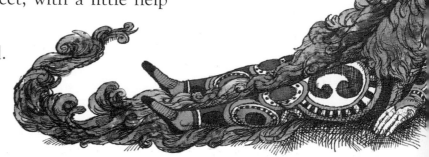

He began to gabble as fast as he could, and with each moment that passed, his eyes sparkled more brightly, his face grew livelier, and he seemed a little stronger, until at last he shouted, "Five, four, three, two, ONE!" and awoke completely.

He struggled to his feet, with a little help from Bedelia.

"Heavens!" he said. "Look how my hair and beard have grown. I've been here for years.

Thank you, my dear. Who are you, and what are you doing here?"

Bedelia quickly explained.

Perian shook his head. "One more crime of Lord Garp's," he said. "We must escape and see that he is punished."

"Easier said than done," Bedelia replied. "There is no stair in this tower, as far as I can tell, and the outside wall is much too smooth to climb down."

Perian frowned. "This will take some thought," he said. "What we need is a long rope."

"Use your common sense," said Bedelia. "We haven't any rope."

Then her face lighted, and she clapped her hands. "But we have your beard," she laughed.

Perian understood at once, and chuckled. "I'm sure it will reach almost to the ground," he said. "But we haven't any scissors to cut it off with."

"That is so," said Bedelia. "Hang it out of the window and let me climb down. I'll search the tower and perhaps I can find a ladder, or a hidden stair. If all else fails, I can go for help."

She and the prince gathered up great armfuls of the beard and staggered into Bedelia's room, which had the largest window. The prince's long hair trailed behind and nearly tripped him.

Perian threw the beard out of the window and braced himself, holding the beard with both hands to ease the pull on his chin. Bedelia climbed out of the window and slid down the beard.

But suddenly, out of the wilderness came the drumming of hoofs, a cloud of dust, and then Lord Garp on his swift horse.

With one glance, he saw what was happening. He shook his fist up at Prince Perian. "Meddlesome fool!" he shouted. "I'll teach you to interfere."

He leaped from the horse and grabbed the beard. He gave it a tremendous yank. Headfirst came Perian, out of the window. Down he fell, and

with a thump, he landed right on top of old Lord Garp.

This saved Perian, who was not hurt at all. But it was the end of Lord Garp.

Perian and Bedelia rode back to Istven on Lord Garp's horse. In the great city, the prince was greeted with cheers of joy—once everyone had recognized him after so many years and under so much hair.

And of course, since Bedelia had rescued him from captivity, she married him. First, however, she made him get a haircut and a shave so that she could see what he really looked like. For she was always practical.

THE TOMTEN

written by Astrid Lindgren
illustrated by Harald Wiberg

It is the dead of night. The old farm lies fast asleep and everyone inside the house is sleeping too.

The farm is deep in the middle of the forest. Once upon a time someone came here, cut down trees, built a homestead and farmed the land. No one knows who. The stars are shining in the sky tonight, the snow lies white all around, the frost is cruel. On such a night people creep into their small houses, wrap themselves up and bank the fire on the hearth.

Here is a lonely old farm where everyone is sleeping. All but one . . .

The Tomten is awake. He lives in a corner of the hayloft and comes out at night when human beings are asleep. He is an old, old tomten who has seen the snow of many hundreds of winters. No one knows when he came to the farm. No one has ever seen him, but they know he is there. Sometimes when they wake up they see the prints of his feet in the snow. But no one has seen the Tomten.

On small silent feet the Tomten moves about in the moonlight. He peeps into cowshed and stable, storehouse and toolshed. He goes between the buildings making tracks in the snow.

The Tomten goes first to the cowshed. The cows are dreaming that summer is here, and they are grazing in the fields.

The Tomten talks to them in tomten language, a silent little language the cows can understand.

"Winters come and winters go,
Summers come and summers go,
Soon you can graze in the fields."

The moon is shining into the stable. There stands Dobbin, thinking. Perhaps he remembers a clover field, where he trotted around last summer. The Tomten talks to him in tomten language, a silent little language a horse can understand.

"Winters come and winters go,
Summers come and summers go,
Soon you will be in your clover field."

Now all the sheep and lambs are sleeping soundly. But they bleat softly when the Tomten peeps in at the door. He talks to them in tomten language, a silent little language the sheep can understand.

"All my sheep, all my lambs,
The night is cold, but your wool is warm,
And you have aspen leaves to eat."

Then on small silent feet the Tomten goes to the chicken house, and the chickens cluck contentedly when he comes. He talks to them in tomten language, a silent little language chickens can understand. "Lay me an egg, my jolly chickens, and I will give you corn to eat."

The dog kennel roof is white with snow, and inside is Caro. Every night he waits for the moment when the Tomten will come. The Tomten is his friend, and he talks to

Caro in tomten language, a silent little language a dog can understand.

"Caro, my friend, is it cold tonight? Are you cold in your kennel? I'll fetch more straw and then you can sleep."

The house where the people live is silent. They are sleeping through the winter night without knowing that the Tomten is there.

"Winters come and winters go,

I have seen people large and small

But never have they seen me," thinks the Tomten.

He tiptoes across to the children's cot, and stands looking for a long time.

"If they would only wake up, then I could talk to them in tomten language, a silent little language children can understand. But children sleep at night."

And away goes the Tomten on his little feet. In the morning the children see his tracks, a line of tiny footprints in the snow.

Then the Tomten goes back to his cozy little corner in the hayloft. There, in the hay, the cat is waiting for him, for she wants milk. The Tomten talks to the cat in tomten language, a silent little language a cat can understand.

"Of course you may stay with me, and of course I will give you milk," says the Tomten.

Winter is long and dark and cold, and sometimes the Tomten dreams of summer.

"Winters come and winters go,

Summers come and summers go,

Soon the swallows will be here," thinks the Tomten.

But the snow still lies in deep drifts around the old farm in the forest. The stars shine in the sky, it is biting cold. On such a night people creep into their small houses and bank the fire on the hearth.

Here is a lonely old farm, where everyone is fast asleep. All but one...

Winters come and summers go, year follows year, but as long as people live at the old farm in the forest, every night the Tomten will trip around between the houses on his small silent feet.

BLUE MOOSE

written and illustrated by
Daniel Manus Pinkwater

This selection has been shortened from the original.

MOOSE MEETING

Mr. Breton had a little restaurant on the edge of the big woods. There was nothing north of Mr. Breton's house except nothing, with trees in between. When winter came, the north wind blew through the trees and froze everything solid. Then it would snow. Mr. Breton didn't like it.

Mr. Breton was a very good cook. Every day, people from the town came to his restaurant. They ate gallons of his special clam chowder. They ate plates of his special beef stew. They ate fish stew and Mr. Breton's special homemade bread. The people from town never talked much and they never said anything about his cooking.

"Did you like your clam chowder?" Mr. Breton would ask.

"Yup," the people from town would say.

Mr. Breton wished they would say, "Delicious!" or, "Good chowder, Breton!" All they ever said was, "Yup." In winter they came on skis and snowshoes.

Every morning Mr. Breton went out behind his house to get firewood. He wore three sweaters, a scarf, galoshes, a woolen hat, a big checkered coat, and mittens. He still felt cold. Sometimes animals came out of the woods to watch Mr. Breton. Raccoons and rabbits came. The cold didn't bother them. It bothered Mr. Breton even more when they watched him.

One morning there was a moose in Mr. Breton's yard. It was a blue moose. When Mr. Breton went out his back door, the moose was there, looking at him. After a while, Mr. Breton went back in, closed the door, and made a pot of coffee while he waited for the moose to go away. It didn't go away; it just stood in Mr. Breton's yard, looking at his back

door. Mr. Breton drank a cup of coffee. The moose stood in the yard. Mr. Breton opened the door again. "Shoo! Go away!" he said.

"Do you mind if I come in and get warm?" the moose said. "I'm just about frozen." The moose brushed past him and walked into the kitchen. His antlers almost touched the ceiling.

The moose sat down on the floor next to Mr. Breton's stove. He closed his eyes and sat leaning toward the stove for a long time. Mr. Breton stood in the kitchen, looking at the moose. The moose didn't move. Wisps of steam began to rise from the blue fur. After a long time the moose sighed. It sounded like a foghorn.

"Can I get you a cup of coffee?" Mr. Breton asked the moose. "Or some clam chowder?"

"Clam chowder," said the moose.

Mr. Breton filled a bowl with creamy clam chowder and set it on the floor. The moose dipped his big nose into the bowl and snuffled up the chowder. He made a sort of slurping, whistling noise.

"Sir," the moose said, "this is wonderful clam chowder."

Mr. Breton blushed a very deep red. "Do you really mean that?"

"Sir," the moose said, "I have eaten some very good chowder in my time, and yours is the very best."

"Oh my," said Mr. Breton, blushing even redder. "Oh my. Would you like some more?"

"Yes, with crackers," said the moose.

The moose ate seventeen bowls of chowder with crackers. Then he had twelve pieces of hot gingerbread and forty-eight cups of coffee. While the moose slurped and whistled, Mr. Breton sat in a chair. Every now and then he said to himself, "Oh my. The best he's ever eaten. Oh my."

Later, when some people from the town came to Mr. Breton's house, the moose met them at the door. "How many in your party, please?" the moose asked. "I have a table for you; please follow me."

The people from the town were surprised to see the moose. They felt like running away, but they were too surprised. The moose led them to a table, brought them menus, looked at each person, snorted, and clumped into the kitchen.

"There are some people outside; I'll take care of them," he told Mr. Breton.

The people were whispering to one another about the moose, when he clumped back to the table.

"Are you ready to order?"

"Yup," the people from the town said. They waited for the moose to ask them if they would like some chowder, the way Mr. Breton always did. But the moose just stared at them as though they were very foolish. The people felt uncomfortable. "We'll have the clam chowder."

"Chaudière de Clam; very good," the moose said. "Do you desire crackers or homemade bread?"

"We will have crackers," said the people from the town.

"I suggest you have the bread; it is hot," said the moose.

"We will have bread," said the people from the town.

"And for dessert," said the moose, "will you have fresh gingerbread or Apple Jacquette?"

"What do you recommend?" asked the people from the town.

"After the Chaudière de Clam, the gingerbread is best."

"Thank you," said the people from the town.

"It is my pleasure to serve you," said the moose. The moose brought bowls of chowder balanced on his antlers.

At the end of the meal, the moose clumped to the table. "Has everything been to your satisfaction?" he asked.

"Yup," said the people from the town, their mouths full of gingerbread.

"I beg your pardon?" said the moose. "What did you say?"

"It was very good," said the people from the town. "It was the best we've ever eaten."

"I will tell the chef," said the moose.

The moose clumped into the kitchen and told Mr. Breton that the people from the town had said that the food was the best they had ever eaten. Mr. Breton rushed out of the kitchen and out of the house. The people from the town were sitting on the porch, putting on their snowshoes.

"Did you tell the moose that my clam chowder was the best you've ever eaten?" Mr. Breton asked.

"Yup," said the people from the town, "we said that. We think you are the best cook in the world; we have always thought so."

"Always?" asked Mr. Breton.

"Of course," the people from the town said. "Why do you think we walk seven miles on snowshoes just to eat here?"

The people from the town walked away on their snowshoes. Mr. Breton sat on the edge of the porch and thought it over. When the moose came out to see why Mr. Breton was sitting outside without his coat on, Mr. Breton said, "Do you know, those people think that I am the best cook in the whole world?"

"Of course they do," the moose said. "Do you want me to go into town to get some crackers? We seem to have run out."

"Yes," said Mr. Breton, "and get some asparagus too. I'm going to cook something special tomorrow."

"By the way," said the moose, "aren't you cold out here?"

"No, I'm not the least bit cold," Mr. Breton said. "This is turning out to be a very mild winter."

HUMS OF A MOOSE

One day, after the moose had been staying with Mr. Breton for a fairly long time, there was an especially heavy snowfall. The snow got to be as high as the house, and there was no way for people to come from the town.

Mr. Breton got a big fire going in the stove, and kept adding pieces of wood until the stove was glowing red. The house was warm, and filled with the smell of applesauce, which Mr. Breton was cooking in big pots on the stove. Mr. Breton was peeling apples and the moose was sitting on the floor, lapping every now and then at a big chowder bowl full of coffee on the kitchen table.

The moose didn't say anything. Mr. Breton didn't say anything. Now and then the moose would take a deep breath with his nose in the air, sniffing in the smell of apples and cinnamon and raisins cooking. Then he would sigh. The sighs got louder and longer.

The moose began to hum—softly, then louder. The humming made the table shake, and Mr. Breton felt the humming in his fingers each time he picked up an apple. The humming mixed with the apple and cinnamon smell and melted the frost on the windows, and the room filled with sunlight. Mr. Breton smelled flowers.

Then he could see them. The kitchen floor had turned into a meadow with new grass, dandelions, periwinkles, and daisies.

The moose hummed. Mr. Breton smelled melting snow. He heard ice cracking. He felt the ground shake under the hoofs of moose returning from the low, wet places. Rabbits bounded through the fields. Bears, thin after the winter's sleep, came out of hiding. Birds sang.

The people in the town could not remember such an unseasonable thaw. The weather got warm all of a sudden, and the ice and snow melted for four days before winter set in again. When they went to Mr. Breton's restaurant, they discovered that he had made a wonderful stew with lots of carrots that reminded them of meadows in springtime.

MOOSE MOVING

When spring finally came, the moose became moody. He spent a lot of time staring out the back door. Flocks of geese flew overhead, returning to lakes in the North, and the moose always stirred when he heard their honking.

"Chef," the moose said one morning, "I will be going tomorrow. I wonder if you would pack some gingerbread for me to take along."

Mr. Breton baked a special batch of gingerbread, and packed it in parcels tied with string, so the moose could hang them from his antlers. When the moose came downstairs, Mr. Breton was sitting in the kitchen drinking coffee. The parcels of gingerbread were on the kitchen table.

"Do you want a bowl of coffee before you go?" Mr. Breton asked.

"Thank you," said the moose.

"I shall certainly miss you," Mr. Breton said.

"Thank you," said the moose.

"You are the best friend I have," said Mr. Breton.

"Thank you," said the moose.

"Do you suppose you'll ever come back?" Mr. Breton asked.

"Not before Thursday or Friday," said the moose. "It would be impolite to visit my uncle for less than a week."

The moose hooked his antlers into the loops of string on the packages of gingerbread. "My uncle will like this." He stood up and turned to the door.

"Wait!" Mr. Breton shouted. "Do you mean that you are not leaving forever? I thought you were lonely for the life of a wild moose. I thought you wanted to go back to the wild, free places."

"Chef, do you have any idea of how cold it gets in the wild, free places?" the moose said. "And the food! Terrible!"

"Have a nice time at your uncle's," said Mr. Breton.

"I'll send you a postcard," said the moose.

PIERRE:
A CAUTIONARY TALE IN FIVE CHAPTERS AND A PROLOGUE

by Maurice Sendak

PROLOGUE

There once was a boy
named Pierre
who only would say,
"I don't care!"
Read his story,
my friend,
for you'll find
at the end
that a suitable
moral lies there.

CHAPTER 1

One day
his mother said
when Pierre
climbed out of bed,
"Good morning,
darling boy,
you are
my only joy."
Pierre said,
"I don't care!"

"What would you
like to eat?"
"I don't care!"
"Some lovely
cream of wheat?"
"I don't care!"
"Don't sit backwards
on your chair."
"I don't care!"
"Or pour syrup
on your hair."
"I don't care!"

"You are acting
like a clown."
"I don't care!"
"And we have
to go to town."
"I don't care!"
"Don't you want
to come, my dear?"
"I don't care!"
"Would you rather
stay right here?"
"I don't care!"

So his mother
left him there.

CHAPTER 2

His father said,
"Get off your head
or I will march you
up to bed!"
Pierre said,
"I don't care!"
"I would think
that you could see—"
"I don't care!"
"Your head is where
your feet should be!"
"I don't care!"

"If you keep standing
upside down—"
"I don't care!"
"We'll never ever
get to town."
"I don't care!"
"If only you would
say I CARE."
"I don't care!"
"I'd let you fold
the folding chair."
"I don't care!"

So his parents
left him there.
They didn't take him
anywhere.

CHAPTER 3

Now, as the night
began to fall
a hungry lion
paid a call.
He looked Pierre
right in the eye
and asked him
if he'd like to die.
Pierre said,
"I don't care!"

"I can eat you,
don't you see?"
"I don't care!"
"And you will be
inside of me."
"I don't care!"
"Then you'll never
have to bother—"
"I don't care!"
"With a mother
and a father."
"I don't care!"

"Is that all
you have to say?"
"I don't care!"
"Then I'll eat you,
if I may."
"I don't care!"

So the lion
ate Pierre.

CHAPTER 4
Arriving home
at six o'clock,
his parents had
a dreadful shock!
They found the lion
sick in bed
and cried,
"Pierre is surely dead!"

They pulled the lion
by the hair.
They hit him
with a folding chair.
His mother asked,
"Where is Pierre?"
The lion answered,
"I don't care!"
His father said,
"Pierre's in there!"

CHAPTER 5

They rushed the lion
into town.
The doctor shook him
up and down.
And when the lion
gave a roar—
Pierre fell out
upon the floor.
He rubbed his eyes
and scratched his head
and laughed
because he wasn't dead.
His mother cried
and held him tight.

His father asked,
"Are you all right?"
Pierre said,
"I am feeling fine,
please take me home,
it's half past nine."
The lion said,
"If you would care
to climb on me,
I'll take you there."
Then everyone
looked at Pierre
who shouted,
"Yes, indeed I care!!"

The lion took them
home to rest
and stayed on
as a weekend guest.

The moral of Pierre
is: CARE!

Index of Titles, Authors, and Illustrators

ACKNOWLEDGMENTS

Grateful acknowledgment is made to the following for
permission to reprint previously published material:

Amos & Boris by William Steig. Copyright © 1971 by William Steig. Reprinted by permission of Farrar, Straus and Giroux, LLC.

The Araboolies of Liberty Street by Sam Swope, illustrated by Barry Root. Text copyright © 1989 by Sam Swope. Illustrations copyright © 1989 by Barry Root. Reprinted by permission of Farrar, Straus and Giroux, LLC.

The Bears on Hemlock Mountain by Alice Dalgliesh, illustrated by Helen Sewell. Text copyright © 1952 by Alice Dalgliesh. Illustrations copyright © 1952, renewed 1980 by Helen Sewell. Reprinted with permission of Atheneum Books for Young Readers, Simon & Schuster Children's Publishing Division. All rights reserved.

Blue Moose by Daniel Manus Pinkwater. Copyright © 1975 by Daniel Manus Pinkwater. Published by arrangement with G.P. Putnam's Sons, an imprint of Penguin Putnam Books for Young Readers, a division of Penguin Putnam, Inc.

Catwings by Ursula K. Le Guin, illustrated by S. D. Schindler. Text copyright © 1988 by Ursula K. Le Guin. Text reprinted by permission of the author and the author's agent, The Virginia Kidd Agency, Inc. Illustrations copyright © 1988 by S. D. Schindler. Illustrations reprinted by permission of S. D. Schindler.

Cloudy with a Chance of Meatballs by Judi Barrett, illustrated by Ron Barrett. Text copyright © 1978 by Judi Barrett. Illustrations copyright © 1978 by Ron Barrett. Reprinted with permission of Atheneum Books for Young Readers, Simon & Schuster Children's Publishing Division. All rights reserved.

"Don't Cut the Lawn!" from *The Girl with the Green Ear* by Margaret Mahy, illustrated by Shirley Hughes. Text and compilation copyright © 1972, 1973, 1975, 1986, 1992 by Margaret Mahy. Illustrations copyright © 1972, 1992 by Shirley Hughes. Reprinted by permission of J. M. Dent & Sons Ltd.

Ellen's Lion by Crockett Johnson. Copyright © 1959 by Crockett Johnson. Reprinted by permission of the Estate of Ruth Krauss.

Flat Stanley by Jeff Brown, illustrated by Tomi Ungerer. Text copyright © 1964, renewed 1992 by Jeff Brown. Illustrations copyright © 1964 by Tomi Ungerer. Reprinted by permission of HarperCollins Publishers.

Freckle Juice by Judy Blume, illustrated by Sonia O. Lisker. Text copyright © 1984 by Judy Blume. Illustrations copyright © 1984 by Sonia O. Lisker. Reprinted with permission of Simon & Schuster Books for Young Readers, Simon & Schuster Children's Publishing Division. All rights reserved.

Horton Hatches the Egg by Dr. Seuss. TM and copyright © 1940, renewed 1968 by Dr. Seuss Enterprises, L.P. Reprinted by permission of Random House, Inc.

Little Tim and the Brave Sea Captain by Edward Ardizzone. Copyright © 1936 by Edward Ardizzone. First published in 1936 by Oxford University Press. Reissued in hardcover in Great Britain by Scholastic, Ltd., in 1999 and in the United States by Lothrop, Lee & Shepard in 2000. Reprinted by permission of HarperCollins Publishers.

The Magic Finger by Roald Dahl, illustrated by Quentin Blake. Text copyright © 1966 by Roald Dahl Nominee Ltd. Illustrations copyright © 1995 by Quentin Blake. Published by arrangement with Viking Penguin, an imprint of Penguin Putnam Books for Young Readers, a division of Penguin Putnam, Inc.

"Mitzi Takes a Taxi" from *Tell Me a Mitzi* by Lore Segal, illustrated by Harriet Pincus. Text copyright © 1970, renewed 1998 by Lore Segal. Illustrations copyright © 1970, renewed 1998 by Harriet Pincus. Reprinted by permission of Farrar, Straus and Giroux, LLC.

"Mrs. Gorf" from *Sideways Stories from Wayside School* by Louis Sachar. Text copyright © 1978 by Louis Sachar. Reprinted by permission of HarperCollins Publishers.

No Kiss for Mother by Tomi Ungerer. Copyright © 1973 by Tomi Ungerer. Copyright © 1974 by Diogenes Verlag AG, Zürich. Reprinted by permission of Diogenes Verlag AG, Zürich.

No One Is Going to Nashville by Mavis Jukes, illustrated by Lloyd Bloom. Text copyright © 1983 by Mavis Jukes. Illustrations copyright © 1983 by Lloyd Bloom. Reprinted by permission of Alfred A. Knopf, a division of Random House, Inc.

Pierre by Maurice Sendak. Copyright © 1962, renewed 1990 by Maurice Sendak. Reprinted by permission of HarperCollins Publishers.

The Piggy in the Puddle by Charlotte Pomerantz, illustrated by James Marshall. Text copyright © 1974 by Charlotte Pomerantz. Illustrations copyright © 1974 by James Marshall. Reprinted with permission of Simon & Schuster Books for Young Readers, Simon & Schuster Children's Publishing Division. All rights reserved.

The Practical Princess by Jay Williams, illustrated by Friso Henstra. Text copyright © 1969 by Jay Williams. Illustrations copyright © 1969 by Friso Henstra. Reprinted by permission of Scholastic Inc.

The Shrinking of Treehorn by Florence Parry Heide, illustrated by Edward Gorey. Text copyright © 1971 by Florence Parry Heide. Illustrations copyright © 1971 by Edward Gorey. Reprinted by permission of Holiday House, Inc.

The Tenth Good Thing About Barney by Judith Viorst, illustrated by Erik Blegvad. Text copyright © 1971 by Judith Viorst. Illustrations copyright © 1971 by Erik Blegvad. Reprinted with permission of Atheneum Books for Young Readers, Simon & Schuster Children's Publishing Division. All rights reserved.

The Tomten by Astrid Lindgren, illustrated by Harald Wiberg. Text copyright © 1961, renewed 1967 by Astrid Lindgren. Illustrations copyright © 1961 by Harald Wiberg. Published by arrangement with G.P. Putnam's Sons, an imprint of Penguin Putnam Books for Young Readers, a division of Penguin Putnam, Inc.

The True Story of the 3 Little Pigs by Jon Scieszka, illustrated by Lane Smith. Text copyright © 1989 by Jon Scieszka. Illustrations copyright © 1989 by Lane Smith. Published by arrangement with Viking Penguin, an imprint of Penguin Putnam Books for Young Readers, a division of Penguin Putnam, Inc.

Virgie Goes to School with Us Boys by Elizabeth Fitzgerald Howard, illustrated by E. B. Lewis. Text copyright © 2000 by Elizabeth Fitzgerald Howard. Illustrations copyright © 2000 by E. B. Lewis. Reprinted with permission of Simon & Schuster Books for Young Readers, Simon & Schuster Children's Publishing Division. All rights reserved.

Wilma Unlimited by Kathleen Krull, illustrated by David Diaz. Text copyright © 1996 by Kathleen Krull. Illustrations copyright © 1996 by David Diaz. Used with permission of Harcourt, Inc.